THE SCANDALOUS LYON

The Lyon's Den Connected World

Maggi Andersen

ARE YOU SIGNED UP FOR DRAGONBLADE'S BLOG?

You'll get the latest news and information on exclusive giveaways, exclusive excerpts, coming releases, sales, free books, cover reveals and more.

Check out our complete list of authors, too!

No spam, no junk. That's a promise!

Sign Up Here

www.dragonbladepublishing.com

Dearest Reader;

Thank you for your support of a small press. At Dragonblade Publishing, we strive to bring you the highest quality Historical Romance from the some of the best authors in the business. Without your support, there is no 'us', so we sincerely hope you adore these stories and find some new favorite authors along the way.

Happy Reading!

CEO, Dragonblade Publishing

Additional Dragonblade books by Author Maggi Andersen

Dangerous Lords Series
The Baron's Betrothal
Seducing the Earl
The Viscount's Widowed Lady
Governess to the Duke's Heir
Eleanor Fitzherbert's Christmas Miracle (A Novella)

Once a Wallflower Series
Presenting Miss Letitia

The Lyon's Den Connected World
The Scandalous Lyon

Also from Maggi Andersen
The Marquess Meets His Match

*** Please visit Dragonblade's website for a full list of books and authors. Sign up for Dragonblade's blog for sneak peeks, interviews, and more: ***
www.dragonbladepublishing.com

CHAPTER ONE

London, March 1814

THROUGH THE MIST, Lord Jason Glazebrook strolled toward the distinctive blue house on Cleveland Row in Whitehall. Inside there would be warmth and life. The levity of alcohol-inspired revelry, contrasting starkly with the dismal exterior of the night was a perfect distraction for a man whose world had fallen apart.

The Lyon's Den, one of the most successful gaming houses in London, offered many attractions and was efficiently run by Mrs. Bessie Dove-Lyon, whose past was mired in mystery. Rumor had it that she'd been a courtesan; others said that she was well-born. She'd married young, and well. Her husband, Colonel Sandstrom T. Lyon from a respectable family, was much older than she and died only a few years after they wed. The enterprising Dove-Lyon had then converted her house into a well-paying business, catering to gamblers, those looking for games of an unusual sort, and those willing to pay a good sum to marry into a good family.

The matchmaker's age was a matter of conjecture; she always wore black and never appeared without a veil. Jason didn't know of anyone who had seen her face. He'd studied her neat form, however, and judged her to still be in her prime.

His brother, Charles, Duke of Shewsbury, disapproved of the Lyon's Den, but then he disagreed with almost everything, of late. Now the head of the family and a stickler for correctness, he had become far too stuffy in Jason's opinion and interfered too much in his life. Perhaps Charles would cease to annoy him after he married Lady Cornelia, although Jason wasn't confident.

Before their father died last year, he had arranged Charles's marriage to the Marquess of Dountry's daughter, Lady Cornelia, whom Charles had yet to meet because a family illness had kept them from London. That might account for Charles's bad humor, although his brother wouldn't admit it, nor discuss it when Jason tentatively broached the subject.

Jason stepped into the gentlemen's entrance of the Lyon's Den where fashionably attired men and women in fluttering silk dresses dallied.

"Good evening, my lord." The attractive cloakroom attendant smiled and bobbed a curtsey as she took his coat, cane, beaver, and gloves.

Jason winked at her, shrugging away his brother's dampening influence. Mrs. Dove-Lyon employed many women, and some, including this one, were a feast for the eyes.

Rubbing his hands together at the night ahead, he passed through the men's smoking room where a couple of gentlemen of his acquaintance were blowing a cloud of smoke, and then entered the main gambling floor. He nodded pointlessly at the silent woman whose face was always hidden as she bent over an abacus in her cage. Faro and Basset were in play, the faro-banks presided over by decorative ladies, the rattle of the dice in the roulette wheel punctuating the strained silence.

Jason stepped into the private gaming room as a loud cheers went up. A friend, Will Denning, his voice raised above the din which centered on Derek Ponsonby, explained how the lucky fellow had just won a handsome wager. He'd bet against Frederick Calvin's ability to ride his horse backward in the saddle in Hyde Park from the main gates to the Serpentine in less than twenty minutes. Ponsonby had failed when he'd become unseated. He'd claimed a foul because he'd been accosted by a park attendant who unnerved his horse, but despite that was now cheerfully paying up.

A footman offered Jason a champagne flute from a silver tray. As Jason took a hearty sip of the chilled wine, Stopford, one of Mrs. Dove-Lyon's staff, appeared at his elbow. "Mrs. Dove-Lyon asked to be informed when you arrived, my lord. She requests an interview with you."

"Oh? Now, why would that be? I don't believe I'm in arrears."

"Madam is in the women's parlor."

Mildly curious, Jason tossed back his drink, replaced the glass on the footman's tray, and left the ruckus behind.

The ladies' parlor was a room he'd had no cause to visit before. Three ladies were seated on the couches. He tugged at his cravat, suddenly wary. The chamber was furnished in too feminine a fashion for his comfort.

Mrs. Dove-Lyon stood to welcome him, dressed in her usual black, and inscrutable as ever behind her veil.

"If you will allow me a moment of your time, my lord," she said in her usual measured tones, "I should like to introduce you to a young lady whose attractive appearance and sweet demeanor is sure to charm you. Mrs. Crabtree, Miss Beverly Crabtree, allow me to present Jason Glazebrook."

"How do you do." Wondering what bee had got in Mrs. Dove-Lyon's bonnet, he bowed to the ladies. Was the woman matchmaking? Jason was amused. He was hardly a good candidate; he would be sailing close to the wind for over two years until he turned twenty-five and came into his inheritance. He had no estate beyond a property in Dorset, and it was extremely unlikely he would ever be duke, with Charles planning to set up his nursery after he married. He would make his excuses after a few minutes and leave.

His gaze settled on the young lady in question. She was dressed in a sprig muslin gown with a ribbon sash beneath her full bosom. Luxuriant golden-brown ringlets peeped from her bonnet, and green ribbons were tied in a bow at one side of her chin. Extremely fine brown eyes surveyed him coolly from beneath gently arched brows. His interest quickened.

"Please be seated, my lord." Mrs. Dove-Lyon gestured to an armchair. "Miss Crabtree is in London for her Come-out. She confessed that she saw you at Lady Fellsham's card party and has expressed a wish to meet you."

Jason took the chair and arranged his long legs over the flowery rug. He didn't flatter easily because he knew his worth, or lack of it, on the marriage mart. He wondered why he'd been singled out. Preferring male company among the *ton*, he rarely attended parties. But he did drop in for a game of cards at Lady Fellsham's, although he had no recollection of Miss Crabtree. Odd that; he was sure she would not have escaped his notice.

Her mother, a thin-faced woman who lacked her daughter's beauty, smiled at him. "Having learned that you are a member here, I gave in to Beverly's wish. I'm afraid I indulge my daughter, my lord. But she asks so little of me, how could I refuse her?"

Miss Crabtree reddened and murmured a denial. She placed a gloved hand on her cheek, which looked soft as a rose petal, and peeked at him from beneath dark lashes. An extraordinarily pretty girl, Jason decided. Even more so if she smiled.

"Some wine, my lord?" Mrs. Dove-Lyon gestured to a footman who waited at the door.

"Thank you." Jason took the glass of wine the servant offered, while his eyes remained on Beverly.

"My daughter has been strictly brought up in the country," Mrs. Crabtree said. "Beverly finds London society a little overwhelming. So, my good friend, Mrs. Dove-Lyon, suggested she might be more comfortable meeting gentlemen in less formal circumstances."

The flush faded from Miss Crabtree's cheeks. Her eyes shyly met his. His gaze dropped to her fascinating mouth. The upper lip, almost as full as the bottom, made him want to kiss her.

"Perhaps we might slip away and allow these two young people to converse," Mrs. Dove-Lyon said unexpectedly.

"For a few minutes only," Mrs. Crabtree said with a slight frown. She addressed Jason. "Mrs. Dove-Lyon has promised to show me a new painting she has acquired. I am an art enthusiast and love to see new works."

The door closed behind them.

Surprised to find himself alone with her, Jason leaned back in his chair and twirled the stem of the wineglass in his fingers. Just what was being offered here? He smiled, his gaze roaming over her, from her excellent figure to her pretty face. "What part of the country do you hail from, Miss Crabtree?"

"Horsham, in Sussex, my lord," she said politely, her voice melodic and pleasing.

"Your father is in London with you?"

"No." Her fingers threaded through her pearl necklace. "Papa is not in the best of health and could not accompany us. He was the magistrate in Horsham, but has recently retired."

My, but she was damn fetching, Jason thought again as she nibbled her bottom lip. The action might have been meant to invite a kiss. It threatened to stir a part of his anatomy, and he crossed his legs. Some debutantes played flirtatious games; others were unaware of the effect their beauty had on a man. He suspected Miss Crabtree was the latter. As marriage was years away, he had purposefully given the young girls who flooded London for the Season a wide berth. Consequently, he was more used to the company of a different kind of woman, one who knew what was what. But this was not a drawing room, it was a gambling club. Which was a different matter entirely.

He bent over to take a small wine cake from the plate. "Horsham? I haven't had the opportunity to visit that part of the country."

Her eyes warmed. "Oh, but you would like it very much, my lord. We live near the river and not so far from Brighton."

"Do you have any siblings?"

"A brother and sister, but both have left home. I am the youngest." She dabbed her lips with a napkin. "You have a brother, I believe, my lord."

"Yes." He disliked Charles's name entering the conversation. "Do you ride, Miss Crabtree?"

She nodded and finally gifted him with a dimpled smile. "Indeed, I'm most fond of the pastime."

Jason popped the rest of the cake into his mouth. He enjoyed the way their conversation animated her; she seemed more at ease. She clasped her hands against her bosom, unconsciously drawing his gaze there.

"Would you care to join me in a ride in Hyde Park one afternoon?" he asked. A few hours in her company could do no harm, a mild flirtation if nothing more. "Your mother, too, of course." He considered it a gamble worth taking, as he'd noticed Mrs. Crabtree tended to limp.

"We keep no horses in London, but we might hire a hack. I'm sure Mama would agree to it, although she doesn't ride. My chaperone, Miss George, will accompany me."

He had not considered the possibility of a chaperone. "Excellent. Shall we meet at the park gates next Saturday at five o'clock?"

"I should like to ride," she said. "I didn't expect to be able to here. I find London a little restricting after the country where one has so much freedom. I do hope Mama agrees."

"Shall we ask her?"

Voices outside the door alerted him to the women's return. Jason rose.

Miss Crabtree's request was quickly granted by her mother, who professed her disappointment not to be able to join them.

He bowed. "Saturday then, Miss Crabtree. I look forward to it."

"As do I, my lord." She smiled, the fascinating dimple appearing once again.

Mrs. Dove-Lyon stood near the door. "You are leaving us so soon, my lord?"

He wished she'd remove that damned veil so he could see her eyes. "Yes, forgive me," he said. "I am promised for a game of faro."

He made his way back to the gaming room, where two men were considering a game of Russian roulette.

One of the beefy, former army bouncers strode over to them. "Sirs, Mrs. Dove-Lyon prefers you play that game elsewhere. She wants no damage done to her premises or her reputation by one of you blowing the other's head off."

"Insolent fellow," a participant in the game muttered. He wove a rambling path toward the door, followed by the other, with the bouncer right behind them.

Jason sat at the table with the three other players as a fresh pack of cards was opened. While the dealer shuffled them, Jason cautioned himself not to imbibe too much. The wine here was always of an excellent vintage, but it tended to creep up on a fellow. Best not to try his luck at Basset. Not with Charles as prickly as a hedgehog.

He forced himself to concentrate as the cards were dealt. His brother would come down on him like a ton of bricks if he was forced to request an advance. He glowered. It was a low blow when his father had made Charles trustee of Jason's inheritance.

Shewsbury Court, Mayfair

SOME HOURS LATER, Jason was admitted by a footman, the porter having retired. His good intentions had somehow come to naught; he was slightly foxed as he mounted the stairs. His attempt to creep along the corridor was thwarted when the door to Charles's study opened. His brother emerged, his hair as black as Jason's and neatly combed, dressed in a silk damask banyan, his firm jaw smoothly shaven by his zealous but disreputable Irish valet, Feeley.

Jason leaned against the door and ran a hand over the stubble on his chin. Curse him, why was Charles at his books at this time of night? He could think of several better ways to spend an evening. He pulled himself up to his full height and stood there indignantly swaying, awaiting the reprimand. "You still awake, Charles?"

"I have not long risen from my bed," his brother said crisply. "In case you've missed it, that light at the window is the sun, having risen from the east." His brother's blue eyes observed him with distaste. "You don't consider sleep necessary?"

Jason's hand went to his disordered cravat and discovered a missing button on his waistcoat. Now where had that got to?

"I do. I shall now, and like all sensible people, I intend to sleep well past noon."

"No, you won't," Charles said bluntly.

Jason eyed him. "I won't?"

"You may sleep for precisely two hours. We are to travel to the country later this morning."

Jason groaned. A tediously long carriage ride to Shewsbury Park in Leicestershire. His stomach roiled. "Oh, Lord, no!"

"As you have been told, Mother expects us."

"Mama won't miss me when she has you there. You are her favorite." He was still bruised by her disappointment in him. "She only seeks an ear in which to relate her latest philanthropic ventures and glean the London gossip, although she makes no attempt to come here and discover it for herself. Tell her I'm under the weather."

"That will bring her post-haste to London," Charles observed.

Jason raked his hands through his hair and yawned. "I fear you may be right." Turning, he waved a hand at his brother. "But I'm not about to waste the few hours I do have discussing it."

"You haven't lost deeply at Bassett?" Charles called before he'd quitted the room. "I'm not in the mood to subsidize you, Jas."

"No, I didn't expect you would be."

No doubt about it, Charles had become dashed disagreeable since he'd inherited the dukedom. As he reached his bedchamber door, Jason calculated the length of the journey to Shewsbury Park and the time it would take, plus an overnight stay. If they pushed it, it was possible he could make it back to London by Saturday.

CHAPTER TWO

Half Moon Street, Mayfair, London.

BEVERLY STOOD BEFORE the mirror in the bedchamber assigned her. The genteel establishment belonged to her father's cousin, Granville, who was away touring the Continent with friends. She settled her riding hat carefully over her ordered curls. A new one made of royal blue velvet, which matched her habit, and adorned with soft white feathers that stirred when she moved her head.

The Cornish maid, Daisy, stepped back to admire the full effect. "The gentleman won't be able to take his eyes off a ye,'ee won't."

A surge of excitement tightened Beverly's stomach. Lord Jason's manners were so pleasing; the smile that lurked in his blue eyes made her sigh. As soon as he was pointed out to her in the Lyon's Den, with the candlelight shining on his raven-black hair, she was drawn to him. But such a match was quite impossible, and her mother had her eye on an older gentleman, a Mr. Williston, who was far less attractive. He had become wealthy solely through his businesses and was known to have a canny eye for investments. He was keen to marry her. She wrinkled her nose. Williston had never enjoyed a physique like Lord

Jason's.

Ordinarily, Beverly held little sway with her mother once she had made up her mind. But Bessie Dove-Lyon, whom she suspected was a crafty woman, had suggested his lordship as a possible suitor. Mama was prepared to risk losing Williston because Lord Jason Glazebrook's brother was a duke. And should Beverly marry him, she'd become a very high stepper. She was informed that Lord Jason hailed from a noble family whose lineage was long and unimpeachable.

A slight shiver went through her as she tried to protect herself from possible hurt. As things stood, she had as much chance of marrying the Prince of Wales. She hated how their relationship had begun with a lie. She had not attended Mrs. Fellsham's card party, as the matchmaker intimated. Lies followed lies, and surely nothing good would come of it. Yet, when she thought of his lordship's eyes alive with interest as they gazed into hers, she still hoped something magical could happen.

"It will take careful handling," Mama said when she sat Beverly down for one of their talks. "Despite paying the woman a small fortune to bring it about, Mrs. Dove-Lyon can only do so much. You must use your feminine wiles to snare him, my love."

"But what if he hears about..."

Mama scowled at her. "He won't. You are to forget about that matter, Beverly. It won't do to dredge it up now, and it should be resolved before much longer."

"All right, Mama." She hated it when her mother was impatient with her. But surely, trying to forget didn't make it any less real. Should she win his lordship's heart, it would be by deception. She took a long shuddering breath. Would he turn against her when she learned the truth? She wasn't sure she could bear to see his expression harden when he looked at her.

For a moment, she considered telling her mother she would marry Williston, who could be managed, Mama said, as he was completely besotted. But the thought of his hands on her made her ill. The exciting prospect of curtsying before Queen Charlotte in one of her drawing rooms, dining with the *ton*, riding a thoroughbred in the park, attending Ascot, living in a fine Mayfair mansion, and retiring to the country during the hot summer months, all served to turn her head for a moment or two before her good sense returned.

Beverly believed she had more to offer than her youthful good looks, but Mama said they were what gentlemen wanted, and she must make the most of them while still in her prime. She was a little in love with his lordship already. It could be said that her feelings were genuine, even if her family was slightly tarnished. She drew in a long, steadying breath. Apparently, she was every bit as capable of moon-gazing as her mother.

Mama entered the room and cast a critical eye over her. She adjusted Beverly's hat over her up-swept hair. "You look very well, my love. Do exactly as I told you, and all will go smoothly. Once Mrs. Dove-Lyon puts her plan into action, his lordship will soon long to make you his, if he doesn't already!"

"Yes, Mama," Beverly murmured, her cheeks growing hot. Her parent had such blind faith in her. But where would it all lead them?

HYDE PARK LOOKED inviting on a sunny day, and today was no exception. Miss George, the chaperone her mother had employed because she couldn't always be with her, seemed a sour old thing, and even more so when on horseback. She rode doggedly beside Beverly through the park gates.

"We shall wait here." Beverly's excited intake of breath drew in the scents of sun-warmed grasses and flowers. She searched the riders trotting their mounts down Rotten Row and the carriages circling the South Carriage Drive. Some had reined in to engage in conversation, and laughter floated on the breeze. It thrilled her, and she longed to be part of it. And why shouldn't she be? An earl had called her a diamond of the first water, but his offer was not for marriage and had not pleased her mother.

"It is past five o'clock, Miss Beverly."

Beverly thought she caught a gleam of satisfaction in the woman's eyes.

"Nevertheless," she said in a firm tone, "We shall wait."

Another ten minutes passed. The horses grew restive. Her chaperone was staring at the watch she wore on the bodice of her riding habit.

"I say, Miss Crabtree!"

Beverly turned to see Lord Jason riding toward them on a glossy chestnut. His hat was tilted at a jaunty angle, his strong thighs encased in riding breeches, his highly polished boots gleaming in the sunlight. Her heart beat faster when he pulled up beside them.

"I do apologize for being tardy," he said with a grin. "Just arrived back in London from the country."

"Please don't give it a moment's thought, my lord," Beverly said. "We were a little late ourselves."

Miss George cleared her throat.

"My lord, I should like to introduce you to Miss George." Beverly gestured to the woman who hovered like a dark cloud a few paces away.

"How d'you do?" Glazebrook barely glanced at her, his gaze settling on Beverly. "Shall we ride down the Row?"

"Oh yes, I have been so looking forward to it," she said.

She edged her horse in beside his lordship's, and they rode side by side while Miss George fell in behind them.

"Did you enjoy your stay in the country, my lord?"

"Merely a brief trip to visit my mother."

His mother. A dowager duchess and no doubt formidable. Beverly was almost glad she would never meet her. She admired his profile with a sidelong glance. "So very nice to escape the city for a little while."

He merely nodded in reply. A man as sophisticated as Lord Jason would prefer the entertainments the city could offer, she was sure.

"I am growing to like London more. It is all very new to me," she said. "It offers far more excitement than the country." She pushed to the back of her mind how much she enjoyed the peacefulness of her home. The slow-flowing river, ducks, and the basket of newborn kittens near the kitchen fire. The wide blue sky and the fresh air. The absolute quiet of the countryside allowed her to think and to dream. How could one do that in London? It was so busy and cramped.

"The days and nights can drag by in the country." Lord Jason Glazebrook raised his hat to two ladies riding past whose sharp gazes scrutinized Beverly.

Beverly watched them. They were beautifully dressed in sober tones with wide-brimmed black hats at a carefree angle on their heads. She grew concerned that her outfit might be a trifle gaudy. Perhaps she should change her hat and remove the gold epaulettes from her jacket.

"Shall we canter?" Lord Jason asked.

"Oh, yes, let's!"

A quick glance behind her revealed Miss George, a determined expression on her face, fall farther behind. When the way ahead was blocked by a group of riders paused in conversation, Lord Jason veered away through the trees. With a laugh, Beverly urged her horse to follow him.

Suddenly, a small brown dog darted out in front of her horse. Her mount snorted and reared as the hound, dodging the slashing hooves, continued to jump about and bark.

Lord Jason rode to her aid, but before he could reach her, Beverly's horse bolted. The mare galloped away from Rotten Row through the trees. Her hat fell over her eyes as she fought to stay in the saddle. Branches rushed by, and one caught at her sleeve.

She managed to push her hat back and found she was headed for a narrow path leading through a thicket.

Lord Jason was suddenly beside her. He leaned over and grabbed her horse's bridle. "Whoa!"

Her mare, responding to his commanding tone, slowed then halted just before they entered the path where Beverly would surely have been unseated.

Heaving for breath and her hands shaking from pulling hard on the reins, she clung on to the pommel as Lord Jason led the horses along a wider path. They emerged into the sunlight. Before her, swans sailed majestically over the breeze-ruffled waters of the Serpentine.

His lordship dismounted and held up his arms to assist her down. Eager to dismount, she leaned forward. Warm hands took hold of her waist as he set her on her feet. "Are you hurt, Miss Crabtree?"

"No, a little ashamed that I couldn't control the horse." Her knees shook, and Lord Jason was obliged to grip her waist again to steady her, which didn't help her much. Breathless at his proximity, she stepped back. She pushed a loose curl away from her eyes and settled her hat on her head.

"These hacks! Pity you cannot have a decent mount." He gave a dismissive nod toward her horse, now placidly chewing a mouthful of grass. "Planned to tip you off in that thicket, I'll bet. I congratulate you, Miss Crabtree. A remarkable piece of riding to remain in the saddle." He turned to secure the reins of both horses to a bush. "Riding side-saddle is challenging enough without dealing with a runaway horse."

"I'm afraid I did little. I could only hang on. But I am in awe of your fine riding, my lord. The masterly way you took control. Why the horse responded without a murmur! I am most grateful. Heaven knows what might have happened if it had been allowed to have its head."

The concerned expression in his blue eyes made her dislike intensely Mrs. Dove-Lyon's instruction to play her cards carefully.

She glanced around. Where was Miss George? She couldn't help but hope the chaperone had lost her way, temporarily, of course. But she felt unsure how to proceed now that she was alone with his lordship. She would have liked to cast herself against his broad chest and tell all. But her first consideration must be for her mother, although the pull of attraction Beverly felt for this man was most unsettling.

"I confess to being a little uneasy about mounting the horse again."

"Have no fear, I will stay close by. But take a moment to rest and gain your breath before we go on."

"Yes. I will, thank you. It's so beautiful here." She leaned back against the knobby trunk of an oak and gazed at the delightful scene before them.

"I can't imagine why you have not married, Miss Crabtree," he said in a husky tone. "There must be eager swains aplenty to be found at the Brighton Assembly."

She thought of the assemblies she'd attended. Mostly husbands of her mother's friends, and older gentlemen danced with her and the green youths who trod on her toes. "Perhaps you haven't been to a Brighton Assembly," she said with a smile. "Most young gentlemen prefer London."

He smiled. "That is true."

What did Lord Jason think of her? He seemed far too smart to be taken in by Mrs. Dove-Lyon. Why had he invited her to ride with him?

"I am sorry your father is ill." He moved close to her.

Forced to glance up at him, she found his eyes were a deeper blue than the lake and held an intense expression. Was he about to kiss her?

She wet her lips nervously. Should he take liberties with her, would she have the strength to push him away? There was no one here to witness it. And where would a kiss lead them? To greater liberties? While she would like very much for him to kiss her, she would hate him to think her fast. An even more distressing possibility occurred to her. Had he an affair in mind?

"You have the most delightful mouth, Miss Crabtree." He propped a hand against the tree trunk and leaned toward her but made no further advance.

Was he waiting for a sign that she might welcome his advances? Her pulse thudded. She caught herself about to lean toward him and raised her chin.

"I believe you wish to lead me astray, Lord Jason," she said, adopting a prim tone.

A humorous light entered his eyes, but he did not move away. "Let's not be formal, call me Jason."

"Surely not on such short acquaintance, sir."

With a half-amused smile, he placed a finger at the corner of her mouth. "Do you know when you smile, you have an enticing dimple here?"

She should chastise him and move away, but she seemed caught, her gaze on his lips. While the desire to kiss him warred with her good sense, an indignant shout broke into her consciousness. Miss George, riding out of the trees on her small gray mare.

"Ah, I see your chaperone has found us." He straightened with unfeigned exasperation.

A scowl on her face, Miss George reached them. "I have been most dreadfully worried, Miss Crabtree. I expected to find you lying hurt or dead on the ground. For surely you would have come to find me once you'd gained control of your horse."

"I was just about to," Beverly said, a little guilty having for a moment forgotten her. "I needed to gain my breath. I am not so very keen to ride this horse again."

"The dog merely unsettled the animal." Miss George frowned at her as if it was Beverly's fault. She managed to ignore Lord Jason's presence completely. "We have been absent for some time. I fear your mother will be concerned."

"Allow me to escort you back to the stables," Lord Jason said.

"Thank you, sir." Beverly approached the horse which eyed her warily.

His lordship gathered the reins and boosted her effortlessly onto the saddle.

Disappointed that their outing was at an end, Beverly arranged her train over her legs. She wished he would smile at her the way he had earlier, but he mounted his horse and turned its head toward the path.

She nudged her hack to bring the animal closer to his and smiled sweetly. "Perhaps we shall meet again, my lord?"

His gaze traveled over her face, then he did smile, sending her heart soaring. "Indeed, I hope so, Miss Crabtree."

There, she had done it. Flirting was not at all difficult. And although she knew nothing could come of it, she intended to enjoy every moment.

Riding behind them, Miss George cleared her throat again.

"I am glad you were not hurt. But we have broken a park rule, Miss Crabtree," he said with a teasing smile. "No galloping allowed. Do not concern yourself, I'm sure nothing will come of it."

He was so attractive when he grinned at her like that, as if she was the only person in the world. "That is disappointing. Under normal circumstances, I find a gallop over the countryside invigorating. I'm sure you agree?"

"I certainly have done, Miss Crabtree," he said soberly. "But I enjoyed today."

As they walked their horses to the park stables, Beverly glanced at his profile. Something in his voice made her want to question him further.

"I trust nothing untoward occurred to spoil your enjoyment of the exercise?"

His troubled gaze met hers. "No, not in the country, Miss Crabtree." He lifted his shoulders. "Something in the past, but no amount of discussion will change it. Thank you for your concern."

He would be as unlikely to confide in her, she thought, as she would him.

JASON TROTTED CENTAUR through the Mayfair streets. Miss Crabtree was too dashed attractive. It was more than that. When he had halted the horse's dangerous flight, the warm gratitude he found in her big eyes drew him like a moth to flame.

While he had somewhat unkindly wished the chaperone to Jericho at the time, her appearance might have been prudent. He would certainly have kissed Miss Crabtree otherwise. But it was unwise. He did not wish to compromise her reputation because he liked her. It wouldn't bother him too much if her mama gave *him* trouble, but he didn't want it to happen to Beverly. She had a keen, marriage-minded mother if ever he saw one. The fact that she had brought her daughter to the Lyon's Den to find a husband had made him careless of proprieties when he should have been on his guard.

His first impression of the situation now appeared to be wrong. Miss Crabtree was obviously a gently reared young woman from a good family, and he urged himself not to pursue her for a dalliance. Especially after he caught the misery in her eyes at the mention of her father. The whole business began to appear odd to him. There was more to this than she was prepared to tell him. He suffered a strong, surprising urge to discover what it might be. It wasn't all about lust, and while it wasn't his heart that drove him either, he did admit that he'd responded to some unspoken plea as if she'd been a stray kitten in need of protection.

Charles wouldn't see it that way, of course. He'd say Jason was up to his usual tricks of wanting to bed a pretty lady. Well, at least he'd be half right.

On reaching home, he stabled his horse, brushed, watered, and fed it. He entered the hall and greeted their butler. "Is my brother at home, Grove?"

"His Grace is in his study, milord."

Couldn't wait to get back to his accounts. Really, his brother was obsessed. Why did one have a bailiff, a secretary, and a man who managed his business affairs for? Jason suspected he enjoyed toting up a list of numbers even more than a woman's company. Or did he have a mistress hidden away somewhere? Jason wasn't privy to that information, but knowing Charles, he wouldn't keep her once the engagement was announced.

Jason paused on the staircase in contemplation of the duchess to be, Lady Cornelia Dountry. He had yet to meet her. A friend told him she was known to be clever, liked to read, and mixed in literary circles. A bluestocking, in other words. It would either be a marriage made in heaven or the dullest thing imaginable.

Jason gained the landing. As he headed for his chamber to change his clothes, he suffered a twinge of compassion for his brother. He hoped Charles would have a score of sons. There was no way Jason would ever want to be duke. The demands of parliament and the running of estates were too heavy a burden for a fellow. And when it was time for him to marry, he would choose his bride. Perhaps Charles didn't want to be duke, either. He had not been raised to be the heir. Their brother, Michael, had been the oldest son, but consumption eventually claimed his life.

As he changed his clothes, he mused about Miss Crabtree and her lovely mouth that he'd been tempted to kiss. He liked to see her smile. She knew of his intention and had been in an agony of indecision whether to kiss him or not, but he was sure she wanted to.

He shook his head. Charles would have his hide if he heard about Miss Crabtree. But what did it matter? His brother had lost faith in him two years ago, and Jason refused to beg his forgiveness. Why should he? Charles had chosen to believe the worst of him. So, they'd reached an impasse, which was unlikely to change whatever he did.

CHAPTER THREE

A FOOTMAN ENTERED Mrs. Dove-Lyon's private room with a tea tray. He unloaded the contents onto the table. Along with the tea service was a tiered plate crammed with cakes, tartlets, and tiny sandwiches.

Beverly wondered who planned to join them. Someone with a good appetite, it would appear. That meant a man. She braced herself for further scrutiny from a possible suitor.

"Now, explain to Mrs. Dove-Lyon what occurred in the park, Beverly," Mama said, causing an anxious shiver to rush down Beverly's spine.

Mama and Mrs. Dove-Lyon stared at her expectantly. Beverly wriggled in her chair. Had she failed them? Was it her fault that after initially attracting Lord Jason's attention, his interest appeared to have waned? She didn't see how it could be anything she had done or said or failed to do. But although his lordship had visited the Lyon's Den on several occasions over the past week, he had not inquired about her.

Beverly did not want the blame to fall on Miss George, who she felt vaguely sorry for, so she omitted the part where her chaperone interrupted them at that precise moment. "I didn't discourage his lordship. It would have been most improper for him to kiss me, so I suppose he decided against it."

She gazed at them in turn, from her mother's pinched face to Mrs. Dove-Lyon observing her from beneath her dark veil. Beverly marveled at how that lady could display displeasure by a slight movement of one shoulder.

"The little Season has ended," Mrs. Dove-Lyon said after a lengthy pause. "The Season will soon be in full swing. Debutantes flock to London, and any advantage you might have enjoyed will be at an end."

"Many will not be as pretty as my daughter," Mama said crisply.

"Most men are not so easily swayed by a pretty face when it comes to marriage," Mrs. Dove-Lyon said. "Social standing and an excellent dowry will trump your daughter's youthful good looks in my experience."

The lady had managed, with one cutting remark, to insult both her mother and her. Beverly felt a surge of anger for her mother's sake.

Raucous laughter floated in from the gaming room. Beverly wondered again why Mama had chosen to consult this woman. She glanced anxiously at her parent. Was it fear or panic that drove her? Couldn't they just go home? Did it matter so much? She might find a perfectly acceptable husband in Horsham or Brighton if it came to that. But the answer came immediately to mind. At home, too much was known about them. The scandal was unlikely to reach all the way from Horsham to the ears of the *haute ton*, although Beverly would still be scrutinized if a splendid match was found for her. When Lord Jason entered her thoughts, desire warred with an increasing sense of hopelessness.

A footman came into the room. He bent and murmured something in Mrs. Dove-Lyon's ear. She replied with words too soft for Beverly to hear. When the door closed behind him, the woman busied herself at the tea tray, pouring hot water into the teapot. "We are to have a visitor. Lord Jason Glazebrook is in the club. I have asked him to join us."

Startled, a flood of warmth rose up Beverly's neck. Her mother nodded with a pleased smile. "Mama, I don't see…" Beverly began.

Her mother shushed her with a frown.

Lord Jason strode into the room, very masculine and out of place in the fussily decorated space. Stiffening with horror, she saw that he looked uncomfortable. "Ladies." He flourished a bow.

"As Miss Crabtree and her mama are here, I imagined you would wish to be made aware of it, my lord. Will you join us for tea?"

His blue eyes sought Beverly's. Was it warm interest she found there or mere politeness? "How nice to see you again, Miss Crabtree." He cleared his throat. "And Mrs. Crabtree. I should be delighted, but I'm afraid I shan't be able to. I am about to take my seat at the table for a game of—"

"They will be advised that you are to join them in a few moments, my lord," Mrs. Dove-Lyon said in smooth tones. She seized a small bell and rang it. The peal brought the footman to the room within seconds. Once the lady explained the situation, she sent him off.

Lord Jason took the only available seat on the sofa beside Beverly. The dainty piece of furniture, with its straight back and spindly legs, caused him to shift uneasily and cross his legs away from her.

"Miss Crabtree was just telling us how much she wanted to visit the Tower of London." Mrs. Dove-Lyon placed a cup of tea on the table at his elbow. She offered him a plate of cakes and sandwiches. "But unfortunately, Mrs. Crabtree is unable to take her. She finds all those stairs difficult with her bad knee."

"You especially want to see the beasts in the menagerie, do you not, Beverly?" her mother asked. "And the ravens?"

"I should like to very much," Beverly murmured over her teacup. She couldn't meet Lord Jason's gaze for fear she would find doubt or even dismay there.

He swallowed one of the tiny triangles of bread and washed it down with a swig of tea. "I should be delighted to accompany you and your chaperone, Miss... er...?"

"Miss George," Mama said promptly. "How kind of his lordship, is it not?" She reached across to pat Beverly's hand. "Imagine how delighted everyone at home will be to hear about the wild animals. You must write a letter to them immediately on your return."

Lord Jason replaced the flowery teacup in its saucer. He declined the offer of another cup. "Shall I call tomorrow at two?"

"We stay in Mayfair, my lord, at number eight Half Moon Street," Mama said with a gracious nod.

He unfolded his long length from the sofa. "I regret you must now excuse me, ladies."

Mrs. Dove-Lyon inclined her head. "Of course, my lord."

His long stride took him to the door, and with a brief bow, he left the room.

"That went well, did it not?" Mama asked Mrs. Dove-Lyon, who managed to convey a level of satisfaction from beneath her veil.

"It might be best if the chaperone gives them some time alone," Mrs. Dove-Lyon said thoughtfully. "Miss Crabtree will require further instruction on how to capture his lordship's interest. And should she be unable to put this occasion to good use, I have something else in mind."

Beverly recognized that expression on her mother's face. She had seen it before when Williston had expressed an interest in Beverly, and it caused a dreadful sense of foreboding in her stomach. She hated the dishonesty and manipulation of his lordship when he seemed terribly kind. Yet, she seemed unable to stop it, and hopeless case that she was, she still looked forward to tomorrow. And not to see the lions.

TRYING TO AVOID the disparaging looks of his fellow gamblers, Jason murmured an apology as he took his place at the table. The banker, another fragrantly perfumed, partly veiled woman, which made the Lyon's Den so unique, dealt the cards.

As he studied his hand, he thought about what had just taken place. The skillful matchmaker had coerced him. He didn't like to acknowledge that he'd let a pair of crafty women put the squeeze on him by appealing to his code as a gentleman. But a glance at Miss Crabtree's face told him she was nervous and not entirely in accord with her mother. He could sense the tension in her slender body as she sat beside him on the sofa. It wasn't what he expected when most girls would have smiled flirtatiously and drew him into conversation, and he found it intriguing. She was unhappy with the situation. He wanted to know why.

Jason tossed out a card. Admittedly, he could have refused. Made some polite excuse, declined the invitation, and left them, but the truth was, he wanted to see Miss Crabtree… Beverly, again. Once he'd realized he was way out of line seeking a flirtation with her, he had tried to distance himself, and over the past week, attempted to banish her from his thoughts. But somehow, she'd lingered, and he'd seized the opportunity to spend more time in her company. An outing with that strict, po-faced chaperone accompanying them could hardly force him into the parson's noose. Nevertheless, with Charles's current grumpiness in the back of his mind, he was determined to be discreet and not allow a whiff of scandal to attach itself to him.

When Gordon Chervil nudged him out of his reverie, Jason threw down a card. "Sorry."

"Have you heard about Harold Simkins?" Gordon asked, frowning at his cards.

"Harry? No."

"He's become engaged."

"He always said he'd never marry," Jason said.

"Well, he is about to."

"Who is the lady?"

Gordon shrugged. "Don't know. Mrs. Dove-Lyon introduced him to her."

"I wonder how that came about." Jason stared across at the doorway leading to Mrs. Dove-Lyon's private chamber.

"No idea," Gordon said darkly. "But Harry doesn't look ecstatic."

"Mm. Marriage, what man does?" Jason asked.

The game ended. He gathered his winnings, said his goodbyes, and went to exchange them for blunt from the woman in the cage. She murmured politely in her rich voice, then pushed a stack of coins across the counter to him.

Jason pocketed the money and left the club. He made his way home to change. He'd planned to spend a quiet dinner at White's with friends and perhaps a game of billiards.

THE NEXT AFTERNOON as Jason was leaving the house, Charles emerged from his study and waylaid him in the hall. "Going out?"

"Yes." Charles looked peaky in Jason's opinion. "I have an engagement."

"Not at that den of iniquity, I hope."

"No." He was glad to be able to deny it. "I am visiting the Tower with a party."

A dark brow rose. "The Tower of London?" Charles asked, his

voice fairly dripping with incredulity.

"Mm. You have the right of it. To view the wild animals and the ravens."

"And who might make up this party?"

Jason continued his stroll to the front door. "No one you know," he said over his shoulder.

"I imagined not." Charles, not finished with him, came after him. "If it's what I fear, for God's sake, take care!"

Jason couldn't help himself; he swung around. "What do you fear?"

"You forming an attachment to the wrong sort of woman."

"And what is the right sort? Lady Mary Smeaton, who spends every waking moment in the stables or on a horse? Or Jennifer Collingwood, who wishes she could go on the stage?"

Charles fought a grin. "It doesn't much matter who it is. You are too young to marry."

A touch uneasy, Jason shrugged. "Who said anything about marriage?"

"Need I remind you that you are the brother of a duke?" Charles crossed his arms and leaned against the wall. "You are, therefore, fair game on the marriage market."

Jason chuckled. "So, you don't think it's my good looks and charm that causes a flutter in a lady's chest?"

"You'd best leave the young lady's chest alone," Charles said with a flicker of humor in his eyes. "It's her family which concern me most."

"Give me credit for some commonsense."

"Do you believe you've exhibited a shred of commonsense in the past?"

"It's just that you don't trust me. Do you, Charles?" Jason asked, prodding at a sore point between them.

"When you prove to me that you've gained some wisdom, perhaps. But until then, I'll be watching, Jas." He frowned. "I'm not about to stand by and let you ruin your life."

"Or leave a stain on the Glazebrook family name?"

"That, too." Charles waved a hand. "Enjoy the Tower. I can't wait to hear all about those animals. And the ravens." He disappeared back into his study.

His brother's bad temper had little to do with him, Jason decided. In all probability, it had more to do with their father's dying wish, and Charles, who was scrupulously honorable, would grant that wish, whether it pleased him or not. And by the looks of it, it didn't.

As he headed out to the street to hail a hackney, Jason tamped down his deep regret for the fracturing of their relationship, the loss of the bond he and his brother once shared. Seven years older, Charles had been the big brother every boy wished for. He'd carried Jason on his shoulders, and later, played endless games with him in the schoolroom when he was home, pastimes which must have bored him silly. Charles taught him to ride, to curry a horse, and take care of it. How to judge good horseflesh by taking him to Tattersalls horse auctions, how to spar, and fence. How to tell right from wrong. To value those things that mattered. It had served him well during his years at university until that fateful day.

CHAPTER FOUR

"I DO HOPE his lordship doesn't feel obligated," Beverly said again as she faced her mother's appraising glance in her bedchamber. "It will be a dreadful afternoon if he wishes to be elsewhere."

"Don't be foolish." Mama retied the green bonnet ribbons at one side of Beverly's chin. "Of course, he wishes to spend the day with you. What gentleman wouldn't?" She tugged at the brim of the straw bonnet decorated with silk primroses and greenery.

"I just wish he had invited me instead of…"

Her mother shook her head. "No one twisted the gentleman's arm, Beverly. You must smile and do as Mrs. Dove-Lyon has suggested."

"I don't like her." Beverly frowned. "She is too devious." She did not add that the woman had encouraged her mother to be deceitful, too. Beverly had struggled over the past months to hold up her chin and be confident, and this made her feel worse.

Mama sighed. "You know we need the woman's help. What with our circumstances such as they are, we do not have the luxury of distinguished relatives or a handsome fortune. Although your breeding is as good as anyone's, and I'll declare that until my dying breath," she added raggedly, sounding as if it might well be.

"Oh, Mama." Beverly hugged her.

She wished she could be as sure as her mother that this was the right course to take. However, expressing her doubts seemed a waste of time, for Mama and Mrs. Dove-Lyon believed they had snared the interest of a duke's brother. A noble family.

She sighed. If only she didn't like Lord Jason quite so much. If only he wasn't so attractive, so wonderful to be with, she might quietly bring about an end to their plan. In truth, her actions were every bit as dishonorable as Mrs. Dove-Lyon's. How weak and ineffectual she'd become of late. She'd been swept along like a feather in the wind. It was just that she hated letting her mother down after all her sacrifices and returning home a complete failure.

Beverly drew on her yellow kid gloves. Perhaps Lord Jason, whom she suspected was no fool, would outwit the lady. But the thought merely filled her with gloom and left an empty feeling in her stomach.

ON REACHING HALF Moon Street, Jason asked the jarvey to wait. He leaped out onto the road, aware of the perilous surge of delight he felt at the prospect of spending the whole afternoon with Beverly and stood, waiting for a gap in the busy traffic to cross to the three-story, red, brick townhouse.

After giving the matter considerable thought, he still had been unable to pin down why he had agreed to this outing. Beverly's doe-like, brown eyes were undeniably lovely, but many beautiful girls had made their come-out this Season. Perhaps because they came from the upper echelons of society, and any attention he gave them would be expected to result in an offer, so he'd kept his distance.

Beverly's family remained a mystery. Shrewd Mrs. Dove-Lyon would have made mention of it had it been favorable. As things stood, there was no possibility of him tying the knot with Beverly. And do what she might, Mrs. Dove-Lyon could not overcome the obstacles that would lie in their path. Undoubtedly, the matchmaker took Mrs. Crabtree's money under false pretenses.

But he had to concede that Beverly was nothing like the usual run of debutantes who had been raised in cotton wool. She had a way of observing him beneath those long lashes as if she understood him and could read his thoughts. A young lady who seemed mature beyond her years, she didn't flirt like other young women, but she liked him, that much he knew.

Despite the main attraction being his family name, he was aware that some women liked him for himself but wasn't particularly interested in discovering the reasons for it. He was not one of those fops preening over his appearance. Neither had his father been and nor was Charles.

Charles! The mention of his brother made him pause in the middle of the street and be yelled at by a passing wagon driver. He raised his hand in apology and darted across to gain the pavement. His brother would be furious, and surprisingly, the idea of making his him angry no longer appealed to him. Even if Michael had died a while ago following a long distressing illness, the pain of that loss still lingered. Jason wanted peace. Although in his brother's present mood, Jason had no idea how to bring that about. He should keep his nose clean, but what was he doing? He grinned. Precisely what Charles would disapprove of.

It was a warm spring day as he mounted the steps to the front door. A maid admitted him to the foyer and asked him to wait in the parlor.

A few minutes later, the door opened, and there she was, every bit as pretty as he remembered, in a primrose-yellow dress and pelisse, a flowery bonnet framing her face. Jason took her hand, breathing in the faint scent of violets which he'd come to acquaint with her. Beside her, her mother smiled warmly. Miss George stood silently in the background, her hands clasped demurely in front. Jason nodded to her, intending to stay on her good side. This produced a slight curtsey, but no sign of a smile. Convinced she was one of those women who didn't like men, he felt slightly defeated. He shook off his unease and greeted her mother.

"Now, you young people go off and enjoy yourselves," Mrs. Crabtree said heartily. "I only wish I could join you, but my knee…"

Beverly kissed her cheek. "I wish you could, too, Mama."

They left the house, and he ushered the ladies into the hackney. Jason took the seat opposite, and the jarvey urged the horse out into the traffic.

"Are you enjoying your time in London, Miss Crabtree?" Jason said with a smile at the chaperone.

"Oh, yes." Beverly fiddled with the furled, frilly, white parasol on her lap. Everything about her was dainty and pleasing to the eye. "I am very much looking forward to this afternoon, my lord. Is this your first visit to the Tower menagerie?"

He drew his gaze away from her perfect mouth. "Ah, no. But I was a mere lad last time. I am eager to see it again."

When their gazes met, hers was slightly quizzical. "I do hope so."

Had he given her reason to doubt it? He turned to the chaperone. "Miss George, have you visited the Tower?"

Her stern look raised a regrettable memory of his governess.

"I have not. I am a student of history, my lord. So much that is lamentable occurred there. I feel strongly that the Tower should not be viewed in such a frivolous light."

"Quite so," Jason said. As the chaperone was now staring out the window, he winked at Beverly. The gloved hand at her lips didn't completely hide her smile.

Dash it all, she reminded him of a sunflower, no, an early spring snowdrop, delicate and pale. "We might stop at Gunter's on the way home for dessert," he said.

Her big eyes widened. "How delightful. I have a dreadful sweet tooth."

Apparently, her penchant for sweets did not put on pounds in the wrong places. He cleared his throat. "I rather enjoy an ice cream myself. Would you care for one, too, Miss George?"

He was surprised when a flush spread over the woman's cheeks. "Yes, thank you, my lord."

Ah, maybe the way to Miss George was through her palate.

When they alighted at the Tower, Jason offered Beverly his arm. Miss George, declining his other arm, strode purposely forward.

The baboons were prancing about for the crowd who threw peanuts into their enclosure. One animal scaled the fence and stole a hat off a gentleman's head. It darted away and hung suspended with the hat tipped over its eyes. The crowd roared. Beverly giggled. She turned to Jason. "How naughty they are. And crafty, too."

"Indeed. That baboon has chosen the finest hat in the crowd, a curly brimmed beaver from Lock & Co Hatters in St. James's Street, if I've not missed my guess. The gentleman looks fit to burst."

"And rightly so. The hat will not be quite as handsome once it's returned to him," she said as the stern keeper entered to retrieve it. She tucked her hand into the crook of Jason's elbow. When she gazed up at him, his heart turned over in his chest.

They strolled on.

A pair of ravens, their wings blue-black in the sunlight, hopped along the ground, taking scant notice of the crowd.

"In Greek mythology, ravens are associated with Apollo, the god of prophecy," Miss George volunteered.

"Is that so?" Jason asked. "I know they are exceedingly clever, having watched their antics as a child."

"They are said to be a symbol of bad luck and were the gods' messengers in the mortal world," she added portentously.

Jason disliked the sour note the woman imbued into the afternoon. He felt sorry for Beverly having this woman as a companion.

Beverly laughed at the antics of an exotic bird hanging upside down on its perch. "Nature's colors never clash, do they?" she asked, her eyes alight.

They were directed to the west entrance where the lions and other wild beasts were kept in a yard. A figure of a lion was over the door, with a bell at the side to call the keeper. Jason rang it, and when the man appeared, he paid the fellow three shillings. They were escorted to view the penned animals, while the keeper explained their origins.

Jason caught a flash of anger in Beverly's eyes as they viewed a polar bear and an elephant chained to a stake. In the lofty, cavern-like dens, a leopard stalked restlessly behind iron gratings, while a brown bear sat hunched and immobile. An African hyena's laugh echoed hideously. There were many exotic species of birds and animals to see. One of the smaller tigers thrust its face against the bars and watched them intently. The animal appeared to be limping.

As they progressed, he noticed Beverly had fallen silent. When they reached the end and the keeper went off, Jason was shocked to discover tears on her cheeks.

"Why, what is the matter, Miss Crabtree?"

"Those poor animals should have been left in the wild." Fury darkened her eyes, her voice croaky with emotion. "That tiger looked so miserable."

Utterly out of his depth, Jason reached into his pocket and removed a clean square of linen and held it out. She took it from him, and with a sigh, dabbed at her eyes. "You will think me a watering-pot! I am sorry. It's just that to see them so…uncomfortable and unhappy."

"No, I'm sorry this has upset you." He suddenly remembered Miss George, but there was no sign of her. Surely nothing less than falling into the polar bear pit would have kept her from her charge?

"Your chaperone seems to have wandered off," he said.

"Oh, no." Beverly's pretty mouth firmed, and she stiffened.

"I'm sure she will return in a minute," he said, surprised by her reaction.

Keeping an eye out for the chaperone, he ushered her to a bench in the sunshine. He removed her parasol from her fingers and opened it. She seemed barely aware of him but murmured her thanks when he held it over her head.

"She didn't mention going to see some animal or bird?" Jason searched the milling crowd. He doubted Miss George would, as she was so disapproving of the menagerie.

Beverly scrunched his handkerchief in her fingers as she watched the people wandering up and down the stone steps. "I fear I've spoiled the afternoon for you, my lord."

"Nonsense."

Bathed in the pale light cast by the parasol, Beverly's fresh beauty and the appeal in her tear-washed, brown eyes drew him closer. He took the handkerchief from her and fought the urge to kiss the tears from her cheeks. Bending, he gently pressed the handkerchief to a tear on her chin.

He handed back the handkerchief. "I sense there is something else concerning you, Miss Crabtree."

Her anger turned to misery. "I shall be perfectly all right in a moment, my lord. And then we must go home."

"So soon?" Surprised, he acknowledged that they should not be seen alone together. He needed to protect her from possible scandal. He straightened. "We cannot wait here for Miss George. I'll send a keeper to find her. If you will give me your arm, I'll engage a carriage."

As they rose from the bench, an elegantly dressed woman of some forty years approached them, a younger woman at her side. Recognizing the lady at once, Jason groaned under his breath.

She paused in front of them and darted a look at Beverly. "I wasn't aware you were interested in the menagerie, Glazebrook. I seem to recall you visiting it once before with Gerald."

"Lady Freemont, Lady Cecily." Jason bowed to the widow whose husband had been a good friend of his father's, and her son, Gerald, a boyhood friend. "Allow me to present Lady Freemont and Lady Cecily to you, Miss Crabtree. Miss Crabtree is visiting from the country and expressed a wish to visit the lion enclosure. We seem to have misplaced her chaperone."

Beverly sank into a curtsy. "How do you do, Lady Freemont, Lady Cecily."

Lady Freemont cast a skeptical glance at him, then turned to further scrutinize Beverly. She eyed the monogrammed square of linen still clutched in Beverly's fingers. "How do you do. Have you grit in your eye? Kind of you to offer the young lady your handkerchief, Glazebrook." Her ladyship seemed unsatisfied with Jason's explanation. "Which part of the country do you hail from, Miss Crabtree?"

"Horsham, in Sussex, my lady."

"That's not far from Brighton, is it? I have been to Brighton, naturally, when the Prince of Wales is in residence. But I have never been to Horsham." Lady Freemont cast an arch look in his direction. "We must not delay, we shall miss the feeding of the polar bear, which Cecily looks forward to. Good day, Miss Crabtree, Lord Jason, please pay my respects to your brother." She turned and ushered her gawky daughter away.

Cecily had not uttered a word, but she never did in her mother's presence, Jason recalled.

"Oh dear, I do hope that she doesn't think…" Beverly began.

At that moment, Miss George emerged from the crowd. "I must beg your pardon," she gasped, her face pale and distressed. She waved a hand somewhere near her stomach. "I cannot imagine why, but I suddenly felt…" Her voice wobbled, then faded away.

"Perfectly all right." Jason felt a pang of sympathy for her and quashed the thought that she might have purposefully left him and Beverly alone.

She appeared genuinely discomforted. However, the damage was done. He didn't expect Lady Freemont to remain silent. This would be all over the *ton* drawing rooms before too long and would likely reach Charles's ears. *Blast!*

"An ice cream will set us all to rights," Jason said, drumming up a jovial tone as he led the two women to where carriages waited for fares. The suggestion seemed to fall on deaf ears, for both ladies were much subdued. He didn't hold out much hope that the afternoon would improve for Beverly, who still clutched his handkerchief. Miss George's face bore a greenish tinge. He decided it was best to take them straight home.

The carriage ride to Mayfair was spent in relative silence.

Jason helped both ladies down from the carriage in Half Moon Street. "I am sorry this has not been as pleasant an outing as I'd hoped."

He offered his arm to Beverly to lead her to the house. "Perhaps I could suggest something more amenable next time, to make amends."

Miss George, apparently eager to go inside, had walked ahead of them. But Beverly paused on the pavement. "My lord, I don't believe there can be a next time."

"Oh?" He gazed down into her delicate face, her soft eyes wide and troubled. Did she feel he was merely toying with her? He only knew that whatever drove him had little to do with good sense. He just wanted to see her again.

"Once again, you have come nobly to my aid. You have been kindness itself, and I remain very grateful but..." She firmed her lips and glanced away from him.

"I can't help but feel there is something very wrong, Miss Crabtree. You seem to be struggling with a problem. I have broad shoulders, should you wish to tell me about it."

She looked appalled, and her arm tightened beneath his hand. "I... no, please. There is nothing, really."

Jason could hardly press her, certainly not here in the street with the maid waiting at the door. He escorted her up the steps.

After he'd left her, Jason returned to the hackney. An empty sensation filled him as he climbed into the seat. By the time the carriage pulled up outside his home, he had come to the view that Beverly didn't want to end their friendship any more than he did. She had not returned his handkerchief. A small gesture and yet, to him, it spoke volumes.

However, he was forced to face the truth. She had come to London to find a husband. And that was unlikely to be him.

CHAPTER FIVE

M RS. DOVE-LYON QUESTIONED Beverly the following day. She had already told her mother how considerate Lord Jason had been, especially about the animals, some of which were most dreadfully unhappy. It had shocked her to see them because she understood how they must feel trapped and presented for public display. Much like she felt in her darkest moments, but she didn't mention any of that to her mother, who would call her sentimental.

She could not do what Mrs. Dove-Lyon asked of her, to entice Lord Jason into kissing her in a public place, although she suspected he wanted to and might have, but for Lady Freemont and her daughter. It had been very hard to refuse to see him again. But the thought of him being trapped into a declaration so horrified her, that she knew she must.

She'd explained to her mother how Miss George had become ill, which spoiled the day and forced them to return early. Mama had been surprisingly understanding and assured her that things had a way of working out in the end. Beverly had never kept a secret from her parent before. But she didn't tell her she'd put an end to this trickery.

Once she was alone, she'd taken Jason's handkerchief out of her reticule and held it to her nose. It smelled of his musky soap and sent a pang of yearning, which brought tears to her eyes. There would be no further invitation. Even as she'd spoken those words to him, which had an awful ring of finality, she'd hoped he would refuse, then declare his love for her and sweep her off her feet. He did not, of course.

Was her mother becoming unsure of the wisdom of employing Mrs. Dove-Lyon's services? She would never admit it and had committed them to this course of action and was determined not to return home to Papa without being the bearer of glad tidings. With Beverly's sister, Anabel, living in Wales with her husband and children, and her brother, Derek, away serving in the Royal Navy, the onus was now on Beverly. As the prospect of her father's disgrace loomed ever closer, Mama grew more anxious to settle Beverly well. And she had been only too willing to seek her future in London to save them from impoverishment. But how naïve to believe that a storybook ending awaited her.

Mrs. Dove-Lyon was not so understanding. She looked sternly at Beverly's mother. "The draught I gave you to slip into the chaperone's tea should have given your daughter more than enough time to draw his lordship into a compromising situation."

Beverly drew in a horrified breath. *Poor Miss George.* How could Mama make her sick like that? Beverly's stomach tightened, and she felt ill, too, with shame, even though they had not told her. She glanced at her mother.

Beverly hastened to placate the horrid Mrs. Dove-Lyon. "We did meet an acquaintance of Lord Jason's whilst Miss George was indisposed. Lady Freemont and her daughter."

"Excellent." Mrs. Dove-Lyon sounded pleased. Her dark veil swung as if in a gentle breeze, while Beverly watched in hopeless fascination. "All is not lost then. It is sure to reach the family's ears. We must act quickly to build upon it as soon as his lordship issues another invitation."

Beverly glanced at her mother. "Lord Jason led me to believe there wouldn't be another invitation," she said in a firm voice.

No relief had registered in Jason's eyes when she'd made it clear they would not meet again. But surely, he must have felt it. What a dismal day it turned out to be. He must have decided she was woefully dull. She drew in a breath. How quickly he'd taken control and found a hackney, ushered the ill Miss George and her inside, and saw to their comfort. She sighed. "His lordship was so…masterful."

"You do like him, Beverly?" Her mother sat straighter in her chair.

"Yes, who would not?" It shouldn't matter now because it was over, but it did, most dreadfully. She'd watched from the parlor window as he'd crossed the road to the hackney. He was her ideal type, everything she looked for in a husband. But she reminded herself sharply that he would never be hers.

Beverly felt certain that Mrs. Dove-Lyon didn't care if she liked Jason or not. She studied the woman, trying to guess what was in her mind. Would she make another effort to try to snare him? Or accept defeat? Defeat didn't seem to fit with the woman who had fought to get where she was in life. The matchmaker might plan to find another suitor for them, but Beverly knew he would fail to measure up to Jason.

There was no other gentleman presenting himself, for Mrs. Dove-Lyon had advised her mother to refuse Williston's offer. He was now paying court to another lady, for which Beverly was intensely relieved. But after letting a duke's son slip through their fingers, Mama would give serious consideration to any gentleman Mrs. Dove-Lyon produced if he was in any way acceptable. And she would try to persuade Beverly to marry him. She would be unable to refuse.

"I don't think we should discount his lordship," Mrs. Dove-Lyon said, surprising Beverly. "It appears he has developed a tendre for Miss Crabtree."

"Oh, do you think so?" Mama gasped. "Of course, he would. A

prettier or more sweet-natured girl he could not find."

Beverly stared at the veiled woman sitting like a malevolent spider before them. Could it be true? Did Jason care deeply for her? Oh, she mustn't believe it! She mustn't! She feared her heart would break in two. Was this some mischief intended to weaken her and make her more amenable? It was right to refuse to behave unscrupulously, and yet, she still suffered regret that she'd lost her chance with him. She chewed her lip until it felt raw and fell silent as Mrs. Dove-Lyon and her mother put their heads together to hatch another plan.

"YOU'RE HOME EARLY." Charles entered the blue salon where Jason rested his boot on the grate and stared moodily into the empty fireplace. "How was your visit to the Tower?"

"All right, I suppose."

"It doesn't sound like it." Charles went to the sideboard. "Madeira, brandy, or a glass of claret?"

Jason sagged into a chair. "Brandy, thanks." He watched Charles at the sideboard removing the stopper from the crystal decanter. He'd had time to consider the events at the Tower and was certain Lady Freemont would waste no time trying to find out if Charles knew. The woman's interfering ways were as reliable as the opening of the stock exchange. "Might be best to warn you about Lady Freemont."

Charles walked across the Eastern rug carrying two glasses of amber liquid. He raised an eyebrow as he handed one to Jason. "Lady Freemont?"

"Yes, saw her at the Tower. I escorted a young lady and her chaperone."

His brother's dark brows met in a frown. "Who was this young lady?"

"Miss Crabtree. She is in London for the Season with her mother. They hail from Horsham, in Sussex."

Charles sat in the maroon velvet grandfather chair. He settled back, sipping from his glass. "Where did you meet this Miss Crabtree?"

Jason had been tempted to make up some story but found he preferred to be honest. He didn't like the idea of lying to Charles when things were so bad between them and supposed he hadn't entirely given up hope that he would see Beverly again. His shoulders tensed, and he took a deep breath. "The Lyon's Den."

Charles sat forward so fast he came close to splashing the brandy on his lap. "What the devil was this debutante doing there?"

"She was there with her mother. Mrs. Dove-Lyon introduced me to them."

"Dear Lord," Charles said in a tight voice. "I'd like to see that Dove-Lyon in the pillory! She is seeking a husband for this girl. Have you learned nothing?"

"I'm well aware that the woman is an unscrupulous matchmaker. If that is what you are referring to?" Jason asked coolly.

"Then why did you…"

"I like Miss Crabtree. I think if you met her, you would like her, too."

"I meet many nice young debutantes. Who are her people?"

"I am not entirely sure."

"It's not difficult to understand what is happening here. Ask yourself why a woman would take her daughter to Dove-Lyon," Charles said crisply. He groaned. "What is it about this young lady that attracts you?"

"Miss Crabtree is unlike most debutantes."

"Meaning?"

"She is not a flirt and does not cast out lures. And she is very lovely."

"Naturally." Charles tossed back his drink and slammed the glass down on the table. "You are aware that they are trying to trap you into a declaration?"

"I am not a fool," Jason said, realizing that he probably sounded like one right now. "I was careful." *But was he? He would have kissed her had he had the chance. What was it about Beverly that made him reckless?*

"You must stop this before that Dove-Lyon woman outwits you. You're obviously not thinking clearly, and she has a reputation for this sort of thing."

"It matters not. Miss Crabtree has declined to see me again."

"Oh? Then she exhibits more good sense than you do. Unless that is part of their tactics."

"I can't believe it of Beverly." Jason raked a hand through his hair. "But then there is the matter of Lady Freemont and her daughter."

"The deuce!" Charles slowly shook his head. "That can't stir up too much interest. Not with the chaperone there."

"Well, the chaperone wasn't precisely in the area at the time."

"Where the devil was she?"

"Miss George had been taken ill. She returned just after Lady Freemont left us."

Charles ran a hand through his hair. "Worse and worse. What do you want me to do?"

"Nothing. I will handle it, Charles. I'm just warning you in case she mentions it, that's all."

"I'll think of something to fob her off. But I don't understand how you could get yourself drawn into this, Jas."

"No, you probably don't, Charles." *You need a heart for that.*

"You won't see the young lady again?"

"It doesn't look like it."

"That doesn't sound like a strong confirmation."

"As I say, I like her very much."

Charles nodded thoughtfully. "There will be many more women

you'll like or even fall in love with before you marry," he said after a moment. "But when you do marry, it will be to the right lady and for the right reasons."

"Have you met any since Lady Drusilla Ryland?"

Charles rose from the chair. "We were discussing you, not me." He strode to the door. His hand on the latch, he turned. "Thank you for confiding in me, Jas."

Jason nodded. When the door closed behind his brother, an overwhelming sense of loss returned so strongly that Jason's throat tightened. They were so formal together. The intimacy they'd once shared was gone. Charles now played his cards close to his chest. He would have once admitted to suffering some hurt about his lost love. Four years had passed since Drusilla spurned Charles and married her neighbor, the Marquess of Thorburn. A better prospect apparently. Michael was still alive and the heir to the dukedom, so Thorburn, whose lands ran with her father's, held the winning card.

If only Charles had found someone else in the ensuing years, he wouldn't be about to marry a woman chosen for him by their father on his deathbed.

Jason cursed. While it did not compare with his brother's tumultuous first love, it was possible his feelings for Beverly could develop into something just as deep. If she'd allowed it to continue. The question returned. Why had she stopped him? What filled those lovely eyes with such sadness? He suspected some distress.

He left the salon with the intention of meeting friends for a ride in the park. Damn it if he didn't want to know what lay behind this mystery. What had brought Mrs. Crabtree and her gently reared daughter to the Lyon's Den when most debutantes were presented and attended *ton* parties and balls?

Two hours later, he returned from the park, determined to find out. Once he'd changed out of his riding clothes, he left the house again. Perhaps the answer might be found at Dove-Lyon's establishment.

CHAPTER SIX

"I BELIEVE WE must play our best card," Mrs. Dove-Lyon mused.

"Absolutely not!" Mama cried. "I won't have my father's name mentioned." She tensed on the sofa beside Beverly.

Her mother looked so stricken, Beverly had to hold herself back from putting an arm around her.

Apparently unmoved by her mother's violent protestation, the matchmaker joined her fingertips to form a steeple. "You must reconsider, Mrs. Crabtree."

Beverly stared at those hands. Long, delicate fingers, the nails well cared for. The sort of hands found on a well-bred woman. She wondered again at Dove-Lyon's past. It appeared that she'd been cast out into the harsh world and forced to make her way in it. Even so, Beverly could not summon much sympathy for her.

"It will encourage Glazebrook to declare himself," Mrs. Dove-Lyon concluded.

"My father crossed my name out of the family Bible," her mother said. "He disowned me when I eloped with Crabtree." Her face flushed hotly. "I am no longer considered one of the Daintiths."

"Nothing changes the fact that Miss Crabtree is the baron's granddaughter," the matchmaker said in dulcet tones. "Come now. Surely you can see the wisdom of it."

It was hardly an ace, Beverly thought wryly. Not when her father's circumstances were taken into account. She stared gloomily into space. It would barely attract the interest of the noble Shewsburys.

At the knock on the door, a footman entered. He spoke quietly into Dove-Lyon's ear. She rose hurriedly.

"You must excuse me."

Beverly watched with interest as the lady followed him out with a hasty step. Whatever he'd said had flustered her.

Her mother sniffed and fumbled for her handkerchief. The usual noise which flowed into the room from the gambling chambers had fallen away. Rising from the sofa, Beverly hurried to the door.

"Beverly!" her mother hissed. "Where are you going?"

"I'll just take a peek." She darted into the adjoining ladies' dining room. Casting a hopefully appealing smile at the scary bouncer who stood guard at the door, she slipped up to the observation gallery. From there, she could view the main gambling floor where a low murmur had arisen.

A tall, broad-shouldered and exquisitely dressed gentleman stood with his cane under his arm whilst removing gray gloves. Seemingly unaffected by the attention riveted upon him from gamblers at every table, his blue eyes coolly surveyed the room. He removed his beaver hat, revealing hair as inky black as Jason's, then handed gloves, cane, and hat to a footman who had scurried to his side.

"Haven't seen the Duke of Shewsbury here before," murmured a gambler at the table directly below her. He sounded disgruntled; his hand paused over the dice.

So, this gentleman was Jason's brother. The duke strongly resembled him, but at this moment, his face lacked his brother's openness and warmth. Another footman emerged from Mrs. Dove-Lyon's private apartments and rushed over, bowed very low, and escorted him inside.

Beverly scanned the crowded room but couldn't see Jason. He might be in one of the other chambers but had not been summoned.

She turned and hurried back to the ladies' parlor.

Her mother frowned. "Where did you go, Beverly?"

"Not far, Mama." She returned to her chair. "I wanted to know what the fuss was about. It proved to be nothing." She folded her hands in her lap and waited as the minutes ticked by. Why had the duke come to see Mrs. Dove-Lyon? Did it have something to do with them? The thought made her cringe, but it would prove interesting to observe Mrs. Dove-Lyon's demeanor when she returned.

"You should not wander in the club," Mama said. "It is unseemly."

Then why are we here? She clamped her lips on the unhelpful observation, while her mother tugged at her bonnet strings as if they choked her.

"Do you know anything about Mrs. Dove-Lyon's history, Mama?" she asked in an attempt to distract her.

Mama nodded. "This house was once known as Lyon's Gate Manor. Her husband, Colonel Sandstrom T. Lyons, died some years ago and bequeathed his family home to her. He was much older apparently."

"So… she turned the property into this… business."

Her mother raised her eyebrows. "One must not look down on a woman for making her way in the world."

Beverly held her tongue.

Close to twenty minutes passed before Mrs. Dove-Lyon reappeared. She walked stiffly into the room and sat down. "I apologize for keeping you waiting," she said in a clipped tone. "Tea has been ordered. We must talk."

Once the tea was served, the woman's obvious annoyance with what had transpired with the duke seemed to diminish. With a brisk gesture, she straightened the cuffs of her black gown and began to discuss the matter at hand. Beverly might have admired her determination had she not disliked and distrusted her.

Mrs. Dove-Lyon cleared her throat. "A genteel widower of some means, a Mr. Purlew, has requested my help to find him a suitable wife."

"Oh," Mama said with a quick glance at Beverly. "Then it's not to be..."

Mrs. Dove-Lyon shook her head. "No."

It was over. A pleasant interlude, Beverly supposed. Although the pain in the region of her heart told her it had been much more, at least for her. She wished she could escape the room and quietly mourn the end of a hopeless dream. But now she must face this Mr. Purlew. She steeled herself to hear the rest.

JASON ARRIVED AT the Lyon's Den the following afternoon. He nodded to the beefy bouncer at the door as he entered the main gambling floor, intent on discovering if Miss Crabtree was in the club. A violinist and a harpist's rendition of a Mozart sonata fought for ascendance above the cries of alarm and gleeful chuckles from the gamblers.

Jason's friend, Will Denning, hurried to join him as he headed for the private gaming room. "The duke came in yesterday, Jas."

Jason continued across the floor. What the devil was Charles up to? "Here to play cards, was he?"

"Cards?" Will grabbed his arm and stared at him wide-eyed as if he'd gone mad. "The duke... join a table to play a hand at the Lyon's Den? I would like a wager on that."

Jason wished Will would leave him alone. "To meet an acquaintance, then, perhaps?"

Irritatingly, Will would not be shrugged off. "Don't know. He was in Dove-Lyon's private chamber. Not there above ten minutes. Left the club straight afterward." He frowned. "Here long enough to hold up play, though. It was low tide with me after that hand. A dashed dampening influence, your brother."

Damn! Jason's ire rose to strangle his throat. He'd told Charles he would handle it. Once again, he obviously hadn't trusted him. How like him to take the upper hand and treat him like a callow youth. Trouble was, Charles had such big shoes to fill, if one took his sporting prowess into account, then there was his first in Mathematics, which Jason had no opportunity to match, having been kicked out before his final year. Jason didn't suffer any resentment for his brother's success; he loved and admired him and desperately wanted to regain his respect.

"Forgive me, I've forgotten a prior engagement, Will." He swiveled on his heel and headed toward the door leading to the street.

"Ha! A prior engagement, eh?" Will called after him. "Going to beard the lion in his den?"

Jason left the house and strode down Cleveland Row. Will was obviously concerned for him but had chosen an unfortunate analogy. Heads had turned to watch Jason's progress as he exited the door. Two and two would be added together by even the thickest skulls to make four. He would be seen to be under his brother's thumb. Charles had ruined the place for him. He hailed a hackney and asked to be taken to Mayfair. He would have to seek another club.

When he learned from Grove that Charles was in his study, Jason strode unceremoniously into the room and shut the door behind him. He faced his brother across the desk. "Why did you go to the Lyon's Den? Was it on my behalf? You had no need. It is common knowledge that Dove-Lyon runs a matchmaking venue."

"It's how she goes about it that worries me. I wanted her to understand I knew what she was up to. She will not employ anymore of her tricks on you."

"You don't think I could have handled it?"

"You seem a little distracted. This closed the door on it. Slammed it shut. Dove-Lyon is a smart woman. She won't try again."

Jason struggled to breathe as rage tightened his chest. "You have no faith in me. You chose to accept that I was responsible for what happened up at Oxford. You took those fellows' word against mine. Why, Charles? Did you not know me well enough to believe in me?"

Charles threw back his chair and stood. He leaned forward, resting his knuckles on the desk's leather top, his brilliant eyes searching Jason's. "Don't you think I wanted to? But there were two witnesses who both swore they saw you go into the boathouse the night before the race. Why were you there if it wasn't to tamper with the boat's steering?"

"Bernie Forbush and Basil Wheelwright lied, Charles. I wasn't there."

"Both of them?"

"Yes, it was they who sabotaged the cox's steering rope, cut it almost through so it came apart during that race between my college and Brasenose. When I overheard them speaking of it, they decided to have me take the blame. I swore to you it wasn't me. You chose not to believe me."

Charles folded his arms. "I bloody well wanted to believe you. But you refused to say where you were that night. You weren't in your rooms. If you'd only told me, I would have gone to bat for you without hesitation."

Jason fell silent. It was true he hadn't offered an alibi. A sense of honor had kept him silent. But now it seemed foolish.

"I was with Professor Chalmer's wife in their residence," he confessed, his cheeks damnably hot. "The professor was away visiting the Delphi in Greece." He bit down on a groan. He hated the way Charles made him feel like a green youth. Well, he wasn't one, and the sooner his brother realized it, the better for both of them.

Charles sat down again, surprise widening his eyes. "You tumbled the professor's wife?"

Jason uttered a humorless laugh. "I rather think it was the other way around."

"Why the devil didn't you tell me?"

"I swore on my code of honor as a gentleman, promised the lady I wouldn't. I knew if I had told you, you wouldn't hesitate to rush up there and make it public."

"I would have had a quiet word in the vice-chancellor's ear. I could have tamped the whole thing down."

"And I would have remained under suspicion for nobbling the boat race, while the fellow who almost drowned, Anthony Fordham, along with everyone else would hate me."

"So…" Charles ran a finger over the handsome engraving on his snuff box. "Mrs. Chalmers had her way with you, a youth barely up from Eton, and then made you keep a promise which ruined your university career. That was your idea of keeping to a code of honor?"

He stiffened. "It seemed important to me at the time."

Charles shook his head. He stood and shoved himself away from the desk. When he reached Jason, he took him by the shoulders and gave him an almost bone-rattling shake.

"Hey!" Jason protested.

He was then smothered by the tang of Charles's special blend of tobacco as he enveloped him in a brotherly hug. "You honorable fool, Jas," he said as he moved away. "If only you'd told me. It's not too late, you know."

Jason watched his brother, surprised by the warmth in his voice. "It is. Those two will back each other to the hilt. Otherwise, everyone will learn what scoundrels they are."

"I understand why you didn't speak out," Charles said. "But will you leave this business in Oxford in my hands and trust me to do what

I can?"

Jason nodded. "I should be grateful, thank you," he said quietly, not confident Charles could fix what happened almost two years ago. But he'd begun to sense a momentous shift in their relationship. He hoped it would continue.

"I apologize for not allowing you to manage this affair with Mrs. Dove-Lyon. But have you considered that it was me she had in mind to target?"

Jason stared at him. "You mean she would try to extort money from you?"

"Yes, if you'd found yourself caught up in a breach of promise suit."

"I can believe it of Dove-Lyon." Jason ran a hand through his hair. "I should have considered it. I wasn't thinking straight."

"With another part of your anatomy? Or your heart, perhaps?" Charles said with a raised eyebrow.

"I don't know. I think she's in trouble. I should like to find out more and see how I feel. Away from the Lyon's Den."

Charles eyed him thoughtfully. "If you can safely pursue this matter with Miss Crabtree, then by all means, do so. Just remember that unlike the women you generally spend time with, Miss Crabtree will expect marriage." He lifted his shoulders. "I'd like to know what has drawn you to her so strongly. It can't merely be the net Dove-Lyon attempted to throw over you. Is it because you have a tendency to rescue those in need? I remember countless times you leaped into the fray to save an animal or the odd person. The maid at the Blue Boar, remember? When she was ill-treated by a customer, you took him on. Fought him at the back of the inn. And he was much bigger than you."

"Beat me black and blue," Jason admitted, remembering the ensuing bruises and discomfort.

He struggled to explain how Beverly made him feel. He'd rescued a young hound drowning in the lake at Shewsbury Park once and had been terribly pleased when Billy not only survived, but decided he belonged to him and followed him everywhere. He admitted he was susceptible that way. But was that all this was? Beverly wasn't in dire need of help like the maid, nor was she drowning. "I just know she is struggling with something, Charles. She hasn't told me the reason, but I plan to find out."

His brother nodded. "I'll go to Oxford tomorrow. I don't intend to let this matter rest. Damned if I will. We'll drink on it!"

Jason watched his brother at the drinks' tray. He felt very much in need of strong liquor. When Charles returned and handed him the glass, he took a hearty swig of brandy, which sent fire burning down his throat. The liquid hit his belly, where it thawed the cold knot, and he began to feel more human.

"Was Mrs. Chalmers your first?" Charles asked, mildly.

"Apart from a few brief skirmishes behind the dairy with the publican's daughter at the Red Lion."

Charles grinned and raised his glass.

He clinked his glass against his brother's. Charles would not have talked of this a year ago. Jason took another swallow as he recalled Mrs. Chalmers's passionate insistence; how she had invited him in on the pretext of freeing a jammed window. He hadn't allowed himself to dwell on what followed between them. Only that he'd left her rooms feeling euphoric, but less than an hour later, became deeply ashamed. He'd liked the professor.

Charles fetched the decanter and topped up Jason's glass. "I hope she was gentle with you."

He shook his head with a wry grin. "Not very."

When he left his brother to his correspondence, Jason struggled to get his head around what had just happened. Charles had given him free rein to sort out this business with Beverly. And by God, he would!

CHAPTER SEVEN

M R. ANTHONY PERLEW joined Beverly and her mother for tea in
the ladies' parlor at the Lyon's Den. Beverly didn't expect
either a handsome or a dashing suitor, and he was not. Of average
height with regular features, his quiet mode of dress and neatly
arranged light-brown hair lacked any devotion to fashion. He appeared
a modest man, as he'd quietly demurred at Mrs. Dove-Lyon's attempt
to sing his praises.

While he talked to her mother, Beverly began to suspect his actions were due more to a natural reserve, for she was yet to see him
smile.

"My son, John, is five years old," he explained. "He is in need of a
mother since my dear wife died as a result of a carriage accident a year
ago."

"Poor boy. To lose his mother so young." Mama tutted sympathetically.

"I imagine your son gets up to all sorts of mischief," Beverly said.
"My sister writes that her son, Henry, who is the same age, is a
naughty imp."

He frowned. "John knows full well such behavior would not be tolerated."

Was there no humor in him? No lightness of spirit? She accepted that this interview was awkward for them, but she relied on first impressions, which often proved accurate. Of course, this gentleman suffered from an unfair comparison with Jason, whose handsome mouth quirked up and whose eyes danced as he talked with her about silly, nonsensical things. She could lose herself in his company, and for a moment, forget they did not have a future together.

Mr. Perlew's hazel eyes observed her face as he drank his tea. She glanced down and stirred sugar into her cup, not wishing him to see the disappointment she struggled to hide. Mrs. Dove-Lyon had said Mr. Perlew received a handsome yearly annuity and was well-connected. Beverly could not fault his manners. But when she forced herself to meet his eyes, something she saw there unsettled her. A lack of rapport. Was she being unkind? She carefully replaced her teacup, fearing her trembling fingers would cause it to rattle on the saucer. His measuring glance seemed veiled as if he judged her, and his thin-lipped mouth added to that impression. Or was she just searching for reasons to dislike him?

"Not every young woman wishes to take on a child who is not their own," he said, those hazel eyes as hard as one of her nephew's marbles, still studying her.

Beverly nodded sympathetically. She would devote herself to any child in her care, whether or not she loved his father. But knew she could never love this man.

Her mother smiled at him as he spoke warmly of his cousin, Sir Abel Richards. It seemed a distant connection to Beverly when the extent of their relationship was made clear. Was Mama so cast down she would agree to such a match?

At last, the painful interview was over. On the way home in the carriage, her mother remarked on the good connections Mr. Perlew enjoyed. "He is able to offer you a secure life, my dear."

Beverly's continued silence about Mr. Perlew's good points had become obvious. While she wanted to reassure her mother, she found herself unable to do so.

A letter from her father awaited them at home. Mama's hand shook when she picked it up from the tray on the hall table.

Concerned, Beverly joined her in the small parlor. She sat on the linen sofa beside her mother while she read the letter. Papa's elegant writing covered both sides of the page. "What does he say, Mama?"

"I'm afraid it is not the news we hoped for." Mama's voice sounded faint. "Here, read it. It's very upsetting."

Beverly took it from her and scanned it quickly, her pulse thudding. The accusation of graft which had forced her father to resign from the bench had not been withdrawn, despite him having been confident that nothing further would come of it.

'Frederick Perkins, the Parish constable,' her father wrote in his flowing cursive, 'has sworn I freed people from serious charges for a handsome fee. It is not true, of course, but they mean to bring me down, and for Lord Paine to become magistrate in my place, despite his connection to a powerful criminal enterprise. I struggle to believe such a thing can happen. But dear Lord, they will have me in prison before you can say, Jack Robinson!'

"Oh, no! Poor Papa," Beverly cried. "How can he prove his innocence?"

Mama dabbed her eyes with her handkerchief. "Do you think you could learn to like Mr. Perlew, Beverly?"

Beverly's stomach lurched. "Let's not talk about him now, Mama. I'll ring for tea. Or would you prefer a glass of Madeira?"

She sighed. "Madeira, thank you."

She pulled the bell cord. By the time the maid answered, her mother, with a shuddering breath, had straightened up and tidied herself. "Your father needs me by his side," she said briskly. "I must return home. I shall book a seat on the Brighton mail tomorrow."

"Yes, we must go back. There is really nothing to keep us here."

"You cannot come with me, Beverly. Mr. Perlew is to take you for a drive in the park tomorrow afternoon."

"Yes, but we can send him a note. Without you…"

Mama shook her head. "Miss George shall accompany you. It is the reason I hired the woman. It is perfectly acceptable for you to travel with him in an open carriage. And I shall be back in London by Saturday."

"I'll stay if you wish me to." It was clear her mother was not about to let Mr. Perlew slip through her fingers. With a sinking heart, Beverly tried to force her features into an encouraging expression. Her mother was determined to see her safely settled before the news of her father's disgrace became common knowledge and spread beyond their town. Would she be forced to accept an offer she detested?

That night, she barely slept as she tried to find a way out of their troubles. If only Grandpapa hadn't made the break so final. Beverly had met him once at a Brighton assembly, an upright gentleman, still strong and powerfully built and hardly in his dotage. His expression had softened when he gazed at her, although he pointedly refused to speak to her mother.

The following morning, Beverly assisted her mother into a hackney, which would take her to Blossoms Inn in Cheapside, where the coach would depart for Brighton. She then went in search of Miss George in her small bedchamber at the rear of the house.

She found the woman sewing a button on her spencer. "Mrs. Crabtree has gone?" she asked.

"She is returning on Saturday."

Miss George nodded. She folded the garment and rose to place it in a drawer. "We'd best go down. I heard the luncheon gong."

Whatever the woman thought, Beverly was not privy to. She left the room resigned that she could not confide in her. She didn't seem to welcome intimacy. Nor was she forthcoming about her own circumstances. Beverly knew that Miss George had been well educated by her father, a vicar, whose living could not support her. The poor woman now needed to make her own way in the world. There were few options for gentlewomen like her. Beverly buried the urge to pity her, sensing she would not appreciate it. She was proud and had extremely strong opinions about a number of matters.

At four o'clock, Mr. Perlew arrived, dressed in a drab driving coat and curly brimmed beaver. His serious mien had not softened on second acquaintance. He assisted them into his black barouche. Beverly, seated beside Miss George, raised her parasol, while Mr. Perlew sat opposite them. The driver moved the carriage out into the traffic.

"I hope nothing serious caused Mrs. Crabtree to return home," he said.

"My father had need of her." Beverly hoped he would not question her further.

"How fortunate then to have your chaperone," he said and nodded in Miss George's direction.

"Yes. I would have gone with Mama had it not been for Miss George," Beverly said, smiling at her to hide her unease. "And it's such a lovely day to visit the park. I enjoy watching the handsome horses trot down Rotten Row with their beautifully dressed riders. Do you ride, sir?" She feared she was gushing.

"I am not a devotee of riding," Mr. Perlew said stringently. "Are you, Miss George?"

"I am not entirely comfortable on horseback. I never feel in complete control. They are, for the most part, rather stupid animals."

Mr. Perlew smiled. "Quite so. How very well put."

Her chaperone agreed with a regal nod. Her hat of brown straw lacked embellishment, and beneath the brim, her expression was set, her mouth prim. Beverly noticed she had a strong jaw.

"Do you hail from London, Miss George?" he asked.

"No." As the horses negotiated the streets leading to Hyde Park, at Mr. Perlew's promptings, Miss George became unusually garrulous.

She talked of the small Essex village where she grew up. Beverly learned how she'd been called upon to care for her brother's child when he was small, but then decided to leave home and forge a life for herself. She was saving her money and hoped one day to run a school for homeless children. "Education frees a child from poverty," she said.

Mr. Perlew beamed. "An admirable ambition."

Beverly had not seen that interested light in his eyes when he had looked at her. It was indeed a remarkable endeavor Miss George wished to accomplish, and she complimented her on it.

As the discussion continued between Mr. Perlew and her chaperone, Beverly struggled to dismiss a faint hope that he would not wish to marry her. She felt guilty and conflicted because Mama depended upon him coming up to scratch.

The following afternoon, Mr. Perlew called for tea. His conversation was again directed mostly to her chaperone. They found much to agree upon, the government's failure to aid the poor and how they'd attended the frost fair when the freezing weather iced over the River Thames last month. The discussion then changed to Hazlitt's review of Edmund Kean's debut as *Shylock* at the Theatre Royal in Drury Lane. Kean was the new Garrick, the distinguished reviewer stated.

"How wonderful to have seen it," Miss George said with a sigh.

"I shall obtain tickets to see Kean in Richard III for the following evening," Mr. Perlew replied with enthusiasm. "It will not be a box, sadly."

Miss George rushed to assure him it did not matter.

They turned to the latest news from the Peninsula in this morning's *Times,* which expressed the view the war would soon be over. Ever the gentleman, Mr. Perlew sought Beverly's opinion, and when she gave it, nodded thoughtfully.

Miss George's cheeks were flushed after Mr. Perlew left. Her conversation at supper was animated, and her eyes still sparkled as they went up to bed. Beverly found it remarkable how much more attractive the woman was just because a man had showed some interest in her.

The next morning, two letters arrived, one from Cousin Granville addressed to her mother. Beverly thought she should see what he had to say. He mentioned his splendid journey through Greece and his planned return to London the following week, accompanied by his two traveling companions. His veiled message was one of hope that she and her mother would be preparing to return to the country.

Beverly anxiously slit open her mother's letter with the paper knife, fearing its contents. Papa was in such a low mood, Mama wrote, that she'd decided to extend her stay. She trusted Mr. Perlew was attentive, and she was keen to hear all about it when she returned.

The letter screwed up in her hands, Beverly was quite sure she and Mr. Perlew were not right for each other. Alone in the parlor, she curled up against the sofa pillows. If only she could have gone home with Mama to add her support. Her father must be most dreadfully pulled down. What else could she do? She wished to ease her mother's concerns by writing an encouraging letter, but she never excelled at fudging, and feared if she put pen to paper, the truth of her feelings would be plain for Mama to see.

That evening on the way to the theatre, and at interval, Miss George chatted gaily with Mr. Perlew. She even had him chuckling at some droll insight. Beverly struggled to join in; she was almost mute with distress thinking only of her parents.

The next afternoon, Mr. Perlew called to see her. She was alone, her chaperone having just left the parlor for her embroidery when he entered.

"Miss Crabtree." He gripped his hat in his gloved fingers as if about to take flight.

"Please sit down, Mr. Perlew," Beverly said. "Shall I send for tea?"

"No, thank you." He perched on the edge of his chair and cleared his throat. "I should perhaps await Mrs. Crabtree's return, but I thought it prudent to tell you this before your hopes rose too high. I've been forced to admit that we would not suit, Miss Crabtree. You are younger than I would have wished and most attractive. Pretty women, from my experience, do not want to live quietly at home. They yearn for excitement. And my son requires the care of a mature woman of sober attitude, you understand." He glanced at her intently. "I trust I have not misled you, nor made you too distressed."

"No, you have acted most appropriately, Mr. Perlew." Beverly studied her hands in her lap, wishing to hide the relief which must show in her eyes. "I quite understand."

He cleared his throat again. "I wonder if Miss George would care for a stroll in the park. I should like to continue the very interesting discussion of yesterday. That is if you do not require her services this afternoon?"

"She is free this afternoon." Beverly rose to ring the bell. "I'm sure she will be grateful of an airing. The early rain shower seems to have left us."

"Indeed. There seems no sign of impending rain."

They waited in painful silence until her chaperone came into the room.

After the two left, Beverly suffered from a paroxysm of emotions. Relief warred with the heavy sense of failure. She had let her mother down. She could not help being what he accused her of, she supposed. But should she have tried harder to gain his regard? She knew it to be impossible. From first glance, he had never warmed to her. How surprising that Miss George had captured his interest. Despite disappointing her mother, she could not help but be pleased for her chaperone.

As she walked around the parlor, she fought a sense of helplessness and tried to discover if any options were open to her. Would her mother continue to seek Mrs. Dove-Lyon's assistance? Surely when Cousin Granville and his guests returned, they would have to leave, as the house wasn't large. There seemed no possible answers. Overwhelmed, tears flooded Beverly's eyes. Gasping, she drew out the monogrammed handkerchief Jason had given her from her pocket.

The front doorbell rang, bringing the maid scurrying down the hall. Fearing it might be Mr. Perlew with a change of heart, Beverly ran to put her head out. "I am not at home, Daisy."

She closed the door again.

The front door opened. Beverly heard Jason ask for her mother. She drew in a sob, wanting so much to see him, but in no fit state to receive him. And what could she say to him? She stood, hands clenched, and waited for Daisy to send him away.

She gasped when, a moment later, Jason opened the door and walked into the room. He calmly peeled off his gloves, removed his hat, and placed them on a table alongside his cane. "Miss Crabtree, how do you do? I must apologize for my disregard for proprieties, I am told your mother is away from Town, but I wished to see you."

Beverly choked. "Yes, Mama has been called to…" A lump blocked her throat, and she couldn't speak.

In two strides, he was at her side. Shockingly, he gathered her to him, his hands on her back. She stood with her arms trapped by his, gripping the damp handkerchief, while she breathed in the musky scent of his soap, limp with relief. She fought the temptation to rest her head against his broad shoulder and confess all, while her loyalty to her family made her stay silent. The shameful details would only send him away, and she wanted just for one selfish moment to keep him here.

Finally, she gathered enough strength to ease out of his arms and gaze into his eyes.

"Come, Miss Crabtree, you must tell me what has troubled you." He took both her hands and drew her down onto the sofa.

WITH A SUPPRESSED sigh, Jason watched Beverly tuck his mono-grammed handkerchief into her pocket. He had made inquiries about Perlew, who proved to have no scandal attached to him. But Jason suspected he was a dull dog. The previous day while riding the park, he'd spied that gentleman driving Beverly and her chaperone down the South Carriage Drive. Jason had not liked how pale and alone Beverly appeared while the other two chatted.

When the maid had informed him Mrs. Crabtree was away from London and Miss Crabtree was not receiving callers, he'd turned to leave, aware he should obey the strictures of society and wait for her mother's return. But then, he'd heard something through the closed parlor door, a soft moan of distress, and gave in to an impulse to see her.

"What is it, Miss Crabtree?" he asked, viewing her distress and deeply concerned for her.

Her large brown eyes filled again with tears. "I… I'm afraid I can-not tell you, sir."

"You can rely on me to be discreet and keep any secrets close," he said, aware that forcing his way in here sorely lacked discretion. "Where is your chaperone?"

"She is promenading in the park with Mr. Perlew."

"Miss George and Mr. Perlew?" An extraordinary turn of events. "I see." Although he didn't see at all. Was the man mad?

She gave a bitter smile. "I'm sure you do not, my lord."

Was she disappointed that the fool, Perlew, had chosen the other woman's company over hers? He rather doubted it. The dreary fellow he'd seen at the Lyon's Den would be hard-pressed to stir any romantic feelings in a young woman like Beverly, but he could be wrong, for she looked distraught. "And has that upset you?"

She shook her head. "I did not feel we suited each other. But Mama…"

"Yes?" He tamped down a deep sigh of relief.

She rose from the sofa. "Would you care for wine or tea, sir?"

"A glass of wine, thank you."

Beverly pulled the bell and returned to the sofa. "You've been so kind. I feel I owe you an explanation."

CHAPTER EIGHT

EVERLY'S SOMEWHAT GARBLED account of her circumstances faded
with the last gasp of her breath. She smoothed the skirts of her
primrose-spotted muslin and gazed anxiously at Jason, who, while
sipping a glass of wine, had not interrupted her beyond an encouraging
nod of his head. Although she had glossed over Mrs. Dove-Lyon's
dastardly plot to entrap him, the implication was clear, and, added to
the unsavory business surrounding her father, he must be shocked.
Indeed, she wondered why he hadn't excused himself and left. But he
was still seated there, regarding her thoughtfully over the glass, and
she did feel a little easier for having unburdened herself. She could
now meet his gaze with honesty.

His eyes smiled reassuringly into hers, sparking a need in her she
tried to ignore. "I can understand your mother's concern to see you
safe, Miss Crabtree, with this affair hanging over your father," he said
with what she considered courteous disregard to the dire circumstances he'd almost been caught up in. "What I don't understand is your
grandfather's reluctance to help you."

"We haven't sought Grandpapa's help," Beverly admitted.

He leaned forward and picked up a biscuit. "Why not?"

"Grandpapa was furious when Mama defied him and married my father," Beverly said. "Once he learns about my father, he would consider his objection to the marriage to be justified."

She watched him bite into the biscuit. Had she lost his friendship? He could do nothing to help her. And why should he try? Her nape prickled at having the horror of her circumstances laid bare before him. She felt very much alone. Providing a small measure of relief to her, at least his lordship now knew the truth. No one could pull the wool over his eyes, not even devious Mrs. Dove-Lyon.

She took a sip of her cooling tea. "So, you see, my lord, there is nothing anyone can do. When Mama returns to London, I shall beg her to take me home to Horsham."

"I appreciate you confiding in me." Putting down his wine glass, he rested his hands on his knees. "The way I see it, Miss Crabtree, we can do one of two things."

Bewildered, she lifted her eyebrows. "We?"

"This is not something you can undertake alone. The first option would be to seek my brother, the Duke of Shewsbury's, assistance."

"Oh, no! That would not serve at all." Beverly's voice grew faint when the image of that splendid figure she'd seen in the club swam before her eyes. So composed, cool, and unapproachable.

"Or, we can appeal to your grandfather. I prefer the second option."

The prospect was every bit as terrifying as facing the duke. If she did that without her mother's permission, Mama would be astonished and certainly displeased. And how might it be accomplished? "Grandpapa rarely visits London. Mama says he prefers country life." Beverly recalled the strong, upright figure she had met in Brighton. His ruddy complexion and powerful shoulders spoke of many hours spent in the saddle riding about his lands. "He wouldn't consent to see me in any case." She paused in thought. "But even should he agree, he will do nothing to help my mother."

"He might feel differently about his granddaughter."

"He barely knows me."

"Blood is thicker than water, Miss Crabtree."

"Is it?" She was inclined to disagree, for here was a man not of her blood, offering his aid.

"Where is your grandfather's estate?"

"Deane Abbey is in Upton Grey in Hampshire...but..."

"You might write to him, but it would be better if you went to see him," he said. "Upton Grey is fifty or so miles from London. Such a trip would require at least one night spent at an inn. More, perhaps, if your grandfather doesn't invite you to stay."

"But I cannot go to Hampshire."

"Well, you could, for I am happy to drive you there. However, you will need your chaperone. Shall we inform Miss George?"

Beverly's head was whirling. "She might not wish to go." Not now that Mr. Perlew had shown such an interest in her.

"Your mother engaged her as your chaperone, did she not?"

"Yes, because Nanny was considered too old to make the journey. But it was to be here in London, not on a jaunt into Hampshire."

"We shall see," Jason said with almost spellbinding calm.

Beverly feared she was losing command of the situation. She should be protesting vigorously. What was wrong with her?

"I believe I heard the front doorbell," he said.

Beverly leaped to her feet, her knees trembling.

The parlor door opened, and Miss George peeked in. She swung her bonnet strings by one hand and ran her fingers through her tumbled curls, her eyes filled with lively curiosity.

He stood. "Good afternoon, Miss George."

"How do you do." She bobbed a curtsy.

"Will you spare us a moment? We have something to discuss with you." He motioned to a chair.

After an inquiring glance at Beverly, she sat down.

"May I offer you tea?" Beverly asked her.

"No, thank you. Mr. Perlew and I enjoyed afternoon tea at the Pavilion." She slid a glance at Beverly and flushed slightly.

"How pleasant," Jason said. "Now, allow me to explain."

It appeared that the matter had been taken out of her hands, which wasn't an entirely uncomfortable feeling. Beverly sank back onto the sofa, aware that she should protest about his high-handed manner, but somehow, she couldn't. She could only stare at him with admiration. Despite everything, hope had begun to lighten her dark thoughts.

MISS GEORGE HAD undergone a surprising change. She appeared quite lively. It must be a different hairstyle, Jason thought vaguely. "Miss Crabtree has urgent need to consult her grandfather on a matter of great importance," he said. "As I am to drive her to his country estate, she requires you to accompany her for propriety's sake."

The woman sat upright in the chair. "I have been engaged as Miss Crabtree's chaperone. I shall not shirk my duty, my lord."

"Good." He smiled at Beverly, then stood. "We shall require an early start. I will call at eight o'clock in the morning. I suggest you pack a portmanteau for several days. Bad weather may delay our journey and extend our stay at an inn."

Beverly rose and offered her hand to him. "My lord, is this wise?"

"Time will tell, Miss Crabtree." He raised her hand to his lips and met her worried gaze. "It is better than doing nothing at all, is it not?"

Despite her obvious doubts, he saw relief and something more personal in her lovely eyes, which made him want to fight for her.

With a bow, he took his leave.

The cool afternoon breeze vanquished some of his inflated self-confidence. What if he couldn't help Beverly? Would he make matters worse?

The urgings of his brain to leave after he learned what lay behind Mrs. Crabtree's eagerness to marry off her daughter had been swiftly banished. He'd responded to a young lady in distress. He felt empathetic towards her, he supposed, because of his own helpless struggle the last two years.

But he couldn't delude himself. A strong attraction to Beverly drove his actions. He'd felt this way since he first met her. He must rescue her from her appalling circumstances and could only hope the baron was a better man than she'd described. Surely, no gentleman would turn away his troubled, young granddaughter.

As he traveled home in a hackney, he dwelt on the worst that could happen. Whether her father was guilty or not, it appeared he would soon be charged and subsequently imprisoned. Charles would be furious when he heard what Jason had got himself involved in. His brother would not be pleased to go from sorting out one mess to his involvement in another of even greater complexity.

He might lose his brother's confidence in his judgment all over again. But he counted on Charles being a good fellow who was known never to turn a blind eye to someone in need. Either way, it couldn't be helped. Jason intended to live his life as he saw fit. He wondered idly if his brother had any success in Oxford. Strange how Beverly's entrance into his life had banished the event, which had occupied his thoughts for almost two years.

If Charles succeeded in his appeal to the university and cleared Jason of any disgrace, it would be like a new broom sweeping away the past, clearing the way for the future. A future he considered to be darned attractive, recalling the velvety softness of Beverly's cheek and her sweet mouth that he wanted so much to kiss. It was the trust in her eyes, most particularly, he decided, which made him want to promise her the world.

Jason folded his arms and watched the Mayfair streets pass by the hackney window. He looked forward to the adventure. However, the journey could be beset with problems if bad weather held them up for days. They might not return to London before Mrs. Crabtree. He seriously considered the result of such an outcome and smiled. He had a possible plan of action in place, which depended very much on Beverly.

And he was seldom wrong about women.

CHAPTER NINE

ONCE HIS LORDSHIP had left, silence fell over the parlor while Beverly tried to make sense of what had just transpired.

Seated opposite, Miss George cleared her throat. "I do hope you weren't averse to my acceptance of Mr. Perlew's invitation to tea, Miss Crabtree, when it was to be just a promenade in the park." She blushed. "The gentleman felt it not indiscreet to tell me you'd both decided you wouldn't suit." She paused and added, "It was my free afternoon, as you know."

"It was perfectly acceptable, Miss George," Beverly said, gaining her wits at last. "The gentleman and I were in complete accord. And I would be very pleased for you, should a proposal be forthcoming."

Her hand flew to her chest. "Oh, my goodness. I don't expect it. I am past thirty now, but I admit, I would like my own home and a child to care for."

"You were living with your brother before you applied for this position, were you not?"

"Yes."

"Surely that would have been better than taking up employment?" Beverly asked.

"No. A spinster aunt's position is not a happy one, Miss Crabtree. I was expected to be there for the children when my brother and sister-in-law were away. But when they were in residence, I often felt in their way. It was not my home, you see."

Beverly swallowed on a swift rush of sympathy. "I quite understand."

"This position the Registry found for me has been most agreeable. Your mother is a generous woman." She sighed. "But I've no idea where I shall go once you are married and have no further need of me."

Beverly didn't wish to think of that. "Surely, Mr. Perlew will realize what a paragon he has found in you." She rose. "Shall we go up and change for supper?"

"Lord Jason didn't mention why you are to visit your grandfather's estate," Miss George said as they mounted the stairs. "I trust your grandfather isn't ill?"

"No, I don't believe so." Beverly paused, a hand on the banister.

Her thoughts had been taken up with consulting the housekeeper who had begun to fuss over Cousin Granville's return, and what to tell Daisy to pack for her. How much should she reveal to her chaperone? Being such a stickler for propriety, she might disapprove and refuse to come with her. She could even write to alert her mother.

"I am in need of my grandfather's advice. As the head of the family, he always provides the wisest counsel," Beverly said mendaciously. "Grandpapa seldom comes to London, so I must go to Upton Grey to consult him." She waited for Miss George to throw an objection into the scheme, and when she did not, Beverly hurried on. "It is good of Lord Jason to drive us there, is it not?"

Miss George frowned. "I trust he is an honorable man," she said. "He might be a blue-beard for all we know. Your virtue could be at stake."

"Oh, my goodness." A nervous giggle escaped Beverly's lips. "Blue

Beard is a fairytale. Lord Jason has exhibited no sign of violent lust toward me. Merely politeness. He has excellent manners."

Miss George firmed her lips. "One cannot always trust how a man behaves. He might adopt a mask to present himself to society. You would do well to keep that in mind, Miss Crabtree. His lordship may plan to offer you…" While her words fell away, the implication was plain. *A carte blanche.*

Beverly had considered this possibility early in their relationship, and although his offer of help surprised her, she could only think well of him. "In that unlikely event, I have only to say no," she said, sounding far more reasonable than she felt, for a romantic liaison with Jason did send her heart racing. "But he is a gentleman, and I have no doubt he will behave accordingly."

Miss George looked unconvinced. "You are an innocent, and therefore have an optimistic view of the world, Miss Crabtree."

"I have you to protect me."

"Indeed," Miss George said with a stiff nod.

Beverly wondered if her chaperone had faced such a situation. It seemed unlikely, but one never could be sure. How vulnerable would one be when sent by the Registry to occupy a new position under a stranger's roof?

"There is danger lurking where one least expects it." Miss George scowled as if they were in peril at this very moment.

"Nevertheless, I trust Lord Jason," Beverly repeated firmly.

She would not believe such a suggestion. She had enough to contend with. But she did wonder where the seemingly sober-natured woman got such ideas. Her chaperone was an enthusiastic reader by all accounts, for she'd mentioned belonging to Hookham's Circulating Library.

Beverly was forced to admit that few women would risk placing their faith in a gentleman of such brief acquaintance as she had done. While she was driven by the hope that her grandfather could solve their problems, her actions were undoubtedly reckless. She must talk to him when they had a moment alone.

"I confess to some knowledge of his lordship's brother, the Duke of Shewsbury," Miss George said, surprising Beverly as they crossed the landing. "He is judged in the best circles to be a highly principled man."

It was curious how she knew this, but Beverly felt it unwise to ask her. "How interesting." It pleased her to know the duke had a gentler side to his nature, although his benevolence was unlikely to include her.

They walked along the corridor to their bedchambers. "I read an article about the duke in The *Morning Post*—that publication is read by the Prince Regent, you know," Miss George said. "The Duke's support in the House of Lords for bills to aid the poor has been lauded." She nodded sagely. "My papa has a bad opinion of aristocrats in general, but he does approve of Shewsbury, when so many of the upper classes don't concern themselves with those beneath them."

"The duke does seem to be of an admirable character," she said, pleased there was something which might allay Miss George's fears. "My Grandmama, who has since passed, was praised for her extensive charity work." Beverly's mother had been very fond of her mama and talked of her often.

The chaperone gave an approving smile before she continued walking to her chamber.

Beverly opened her door, astonished at how much a smile could soften a person's face. Perhaps their journey would not be as awkward as she'd feared. At least not until they arrived at Deane Abbey.

She greeted the maid, who stood waiting for her. "Pack a portmanteau, Daisy. Miss George and I are to travel to the country tomorrow. Lord Jason Glazebrook will be escorting us to Upton Grey."

"Oh me goodness!" Daisy's freckled face beamed. "Ye are travelin' with that handsome gentleman, Miss Beverly?"

Beverly smiled at the maid, who was new to London from the country, and busied herself with considering what to select. She wanted to look her best. "We must pack enough for several days. The green-spotted muslin and the primrose spencer. I shall wear the lilac carriage gown, which goes so well with my gray pelisse."

As she considered her choice of bonnets, her thoughts turned unwillingly to their ultimate destination. What if her grandfather refused to see her? She might have written, but that would take too long. If the worst happened, she expected Jason to appeal to his brother, which would, no doubt, fall on deaf ears. Hadn't the duke come specifically to the Lyon's Den to stop his brother from becoming involved with her?

While she examined her kid half-boots for signs of wear, she acknowledged that she'd allowed Jason to overwhelm her good sense. There was a fluttery feeling in her stomach as sadness mixed with excitement at the prospect of being near him, while she knew he could never be hers.

By MIDMORNING, THE chaise, driven by two postboys, left the ramshackle outskirts of London behind. Jason rode beside them, mounted on his horse, Centaur. He'd considered it best for propriety's sake not to hire a coach. They made good time, bowling along the toll road at a brisk pace through the Surrey countryside, passing through woodlands of beech, ash, and larch decked out in spring finery, while the scents of wildflowers filled the air.

The two ladies, charmingly attired in their traveling apparel, chatted to him when he brought his mount close. They were to stop for luncheon at the inn in Camberley, where Charles kept horses. As they slowed the team on the rise of the turnpike road through Bagshot Heath, Miss George beckoned from the window. "Is there any chance we might encounter highwaymen, Lord Jason? I remember reading this area had been rife with them."

"You refer, I believe, to William Davies, or 'the Golden Farmer,' as he was called," Jason said. "He robbed the coaches around here back in the seventeenth century. A genteel robber, he was known to treat his victims politely with the greeting 'Pray ladies, don't be frightened. I am in distress and money I must have.'" Jason smiled at the chaperone. "Rest assured, Miss George, no robbers have been operating in this vicinity since Davies was hanged." He patted the Manton's pistol in his pocket. "In any event, I have come armed."

"Oh! That is most comforting, sir," Miss George called after him. "You would teach those rascals a lesson, I am sure."

His smiling eyes sought Beverly's, but she looked down to hide the amusement he'd seen in them. He sought instead to distract the chaperone, by pointing out an obelisk in the distance, a brick tower built on the top of the knoll. Then the horses were urged to increase their pace while Jason rode ahead.

A half-hour later, Jason dismounted at the White Hart Inn and instructed the groom to see to his horse. He kicked the dust from his top-boots and shed his riding coat as the chaise drove into the forecourt.

While the team was replaced with the duke's horses, they ordered luncheon. When Miss George went to freshen up, Jason, noting the faint crease marring Beverly's brow, put a hand on her arm to delay her from following the chaperone from the room. "Do you regret your decision to come? Should I not have encouraged you?"

"I wanted to come." Her cheeks grew pink. "But I admit to a measure of uneasiness should Grandpapa fail to admit us." Her eyes searched his. "But how can I not be grateful to you when you've been so generous?"

"I don't want your gratitude," he said urgently, disliking the tension in her slender body. "I hope for more than that."

Her eyes widened. "I...I am sorry, my lord," she said, after a pause. "If I've given you the impression that I might...that you..." She caught her lip between her teeth. "Please understand that I have no intentions beyond friendship. I must go and remove the travel dust, for they will shortly bring our meals." She hurried away before he could say anything further.

Lord, she almost ran from the room. He had been damnably clumsy. What the devil was he doing declaring himself in a public dining room? It was only because he wanted to banish the anxiety in her eyes. To make her believe she could lean on him. But he didn't want to be just a friend. He wanted to have her in his arms, and it was becoming increasingly difficult not to act on it.

He must be losing his mind. He had no home to offer for years, his property being tenanted and tied up in the trust. It was exceedingly doubtful Charles would give his blessing to the marriage, nor would he agree to break the trust, should it be within his power to do so. Jason realized he wasn't entirely sure what his brother would agree to. It hardly mattered, for unless Charles had some success in Oxford, Jason didn't feel worthy of asking Beverly for her hand.

The waiter entered and placed a tankard of ale on the table before him. Dash it all! Modesty hadn't sent Beverly scurrying away. She was repelled by his blunt declaration. He'd been confident she felt as he did. That she might care for him a little. It appeared he was wrong. He sat at the table and took a long draught from the tankard, failing to taste it. He'd appreciated her honesty with him about her circumstances. Was she being completely honest now? He put down the ale, spilling froth onto the table. Whether she cared for him or not, he would do what he set out to do and see her happy. For some other man to claim, he thought, clamping his teeth.

CHAPTER TEN

"M ISS CRABTREE, YOU appear a trifle flustered," Miss George observed as they met on the stairs.

"It is a little too warm in the parlor." Beverly sidestepped her.

Not to be denied, Miss George followed. "Did Lord Jason say something to upset you? I warned you his intentions may not be honorable."

"He could hardly make advances to me in a dining room, Miss George." The woman was like a hound on the scent of a fox. The fact that she was uncomfortably close to the truth only made it worse.

Her chaperone frowned. "It is my duty. Mrs. Crabtree has placed her trust in me, and I shall not fail her."

Her virtue could not be in safer hands; even a Bow Street Runner could do no better. Beverly forced a smile, aware she'd hurt the woman's feelings. "I do appreciate your concern, but it's really not necessary. I must tidy myself. Please go down. Our meals will soon be brought to us." Beverly scurried past her.

In the privy, Beverly peered into the small mirror she carried in her reticule as she tried to tidy her hair. Lord Jason must have meant a liaison. How could it be otherwise, with the duke so vehemently against the match that he would come to the Lyon's Den to put an end to it?

Miss George was right; she was naïve. She must have unwittingly led him to believe she would agree to a dalliance. Tears filled her eyes. She dashed them away and wished she didn't love him, didn't want him so much it made her heart hurt. But didn't her wise nanny always say that it was foolish to ask for the moon?

When she returned to the dining room, their meals waited untouched on the table. Jason's serious eyes sought hers as he came to pull out her chair.

Unable to look at him, Beverly smiled at Miss George. "I am sorry I've kept you both waiting. I do hope the food hasn't grown cold."

He eased in her chair and returned to his own. Seating himself, he reached for the wine carafe and poured her a glass. "We should reach Upton Grey by early evening," he said, sounding oddly solemn. "Will you go directly to your grandfather, Miss Crabtree?"

With an effort, Beverly's gaze met his. She trembled at the passionate look he cast her, one at odds with his tone. Her pulse raced, and for a moment, the noise around the room seemed to fade. "We are making excellent time!" she said, her voice brittle to her ears. "How fortunate we have been with the weather. We'll spend the night at the village inn. I'll visit my grandfather in the morning."

Miss George started. "Surely, I will accompany you, Miss Crabtree. Appearances must be upheld."

"Of course. Grandpapa will wish to meet you." What would he make of them? She must ask Jason to distract her chaperone and allow her time alone to say her piece to her grandfather. She prodded the flaky pastry of her chicken pie, her stomach tied in knots as she forked up a piece of meat. Despite her efforts not to, she had come to rely on him far too much, but she could not bear to think of her life when he was gone from it.

After the meal, there was no chance for conversation. They were swept out into the carriage again and back on the road.

Beverly chatted aimlessly with Miss George as the miles passed. She flicked more than one anxious glance at Jason when he angled his horse alongside them. He frowned in thought, seemingly preoccupied. Had she disappointed him?

The rest of their journey took them through the beautiful, undulating Hampshire countryside, dotted with churches, small farmhouses, cottages, and endless green meadows.

As the sun sank behind the trees in the west, the carriage rolled past farm buildings and small thatched cottages. Then they negotiated a sharp turn around the village pond. Through the window, Beverly viewed the village her mother grew up in. She knew it so well; she felt as if she'd grown up here, too. Upton Grey had been brought alive by her mother's sorrowful reminiscences. The carriage rattled past the blacksmith's shop, the Scotch pines beside the church, and the rectory in its well-kept garden.

They pulled into the Fox and Goose's forecourt, and the ostler hurried out in the dim light to see to the horses. Jason escorted them inside while their baggage was removed from the carriage. Leaving him to speak to the innkeeper, a housemaid took Beverly and Miss George to the chamber they were to share.

"Well, here we are at last, Miss Crabtree," Miss George said as their bags, bandboxes, and portmanteau were brought in by the boot boy. "You will soon be with your grandfather."

"Yes, I am eager to see him." Beverly forced a smile. While trepidation tightened her chest, she shook out the creases in the muslin dress she planned to wear at dinner.

After an excellent meal, which Beverly barely tasted, they retired to the busy inn parlor for a game of cards by the fireside. Under Miss George's disapproving gaze, Beverly indulged in two glasses of the fruity wine. With the fire warming her, she gazed sleepy-eyed at the handsome man opposite and put down the wrong card again.

He grinned at her. "I'm not sure you meant to do that, Miss Crabtree."

She straightened quickly, aware she'd been admiring his mouth. "Oh? Would you please excuse me?" She laid down her cards, putting an end to their game. "It's been a long day. I suppose I am a little weary." She was more strung up than tired, taut as wire, while questions with no conceivable answers flooded her mind. What lay ahead tomorrow? Would Grandpapa take her in? Would he send Jason away? Might she never see the man she loved again?

"It's a good thing we were not playing for money," Jason observed. "What say you, Miss George? Shall we call it a night?" When the chaperone assented, he gathered up the cards and put them away.

Miss George excused herself to go and make sure their chamber was made ready for them.

After she'd left the room, Jason reached across the table and placed his hand over Beverly's. He smiled and squeezed it gently. "I look forward to meeting your grandfather. The innkeeper is a chatty fellow. He told me the barony was awarded to your ancestor by King Charles II for his support during the civil war. The abbey is impressive by all accounts."

Startled by the touch of his large, warm hand on hers, she drew away, feeling the heat rise to her face. "Yes, that is true, although I've never seen the abbey myself. Hasn't it grown warm in here? I don't see why we must have a roaring fire on such a mild evening."

"A disgraceful extravagance," he agreed, a hint of a smile in his blue eyes.

She smiled back, admiring the way his hair curled at his temples. "I believe I'll have another glass of wine."

He raised an amused eyebrow. "Coffee might be a better choice."

She lifted her chin. "One more glass cannot hurt."

"You might feel differently tomorrow." He poured a half glass for her from the carafe.

She took it from him and drank, the wine easing her tension. "Tomorrow, I must speak to Grandpapa alone."

"I'll take care of Miss George." His expression clouded. "I'm sorry about what I said earlier. I fear it might have been unwelcome."

"Oh, that," she said with a casual lift of her shoulders. "I am not upset. In fact, I am rather flattered." She cleared her throat, aware the wine had loosened her tongue, but determined to take this opportunity to give voice to her thoughts.

He sat back in his chair. "Flattered?"

"Yes, that a gentleman such as you, who must have known many women, would wish to…to…invite me to…" She paused, aware there were people seated around the room, playing backgammon or card games. One lady was knitting, her needles flashing while her gaze rested on Beverly.

His eyes widened. "I don't believe—"

Miss George appeared beside the table. "I've taken the precaution of ordering warming pans to be placed in our beds, Miss Crabtree."

Caught by the consternation on his handsome face, Beverly had been intent on finding the right words to explain herself and hadn't noticed the chaperone's approach. "How thoughtful, thank you."

Miss George nodded assertively. "The sheets are often damp in inns. One might catch one's death if precautions are not taken."

"Yes, quite so," Beverly agreed, her voice faint.

Although Jason had risen to assist the woman into her chair, she pointedly remained standing.

Forced to rise, Beverly offered her hand to him. "I shall say goodnight, sir. Thank you for bringing us here safely and in such fine style."

His long fingers closed over hers for a moment, then he bowed. "The pleasure has been all mine. Miss Crabtree, Miss George. Goodnight."

Beverly followed the chaperone from the room. If Grandpapa took her in, there might not be another chance to talk to Jason alone. She glanced back, but he was staring into the fire, the wine glass in his hand. Tomorrow would bring an end to her dreams, but despite the knowledge they had no future together, her heart refused to give up.

JASON TURNED FROM the fire as Beverly disappeared from the room. He signaled to the waiter for another bottle. While his rampant desire was to get completely bosky, he cautioned himself to go carefully. It wouldn't do to be the worst for wear tomorrow. And he needed his mind working clearly. What did Miss Crabtree think he asked of her? To become his mistress? What on earth had he said to give her that impression? He went over their earlier conversation. It was true he hadn't been able to declare his intentions. Dear Lord, did she think him capable of such a low act that he would treat her so shabbily? The recollection that he had considered a brief liaison when they first met was quickly thrust away. He took a deep sip of wine. She did, apparently, and right now, there wasn't a thing he could do about it.

It was past midnight when he finally settled into bed. He lay staring into the darkness while his busy mind worked for an answer to repair the damage he'd done.

The door opened, spilling candlelight into the room from the corridor.

What the devil! Jason sat up, searching for his pistol beneath his pillow.

"Lord Jason?"

"What on earth… Miss Crabtree?"

Jason leaped from the bed, taking the sheet with him to cover his nakedness. He struck a taper and lit a candle.

"I must speak to you." She slipped into the room and closed the door.

"Well, you can't. Good grief. Not here. What if someone hears us? These walls are paper-thin."

She took a tentative step into the room.

"Stay right there," he ordered as he hunted for his banyan in the pile of clothes on the chair. Valets were annoying but damn necessary. He found the silk damask garment and shrugged awkwardly into it, then dropped the sheet. "Now." He tied the sash, sounding brisker than he felt. "Tell me what has brought you here. Has something happened to Miss George?"

"Miss George is asleep. She snores most dreadfully."

"And that is why you've come?" he asked inanely, fearing all the blood had abandoned his brains for a more demanding part of his anatomy. Beverly, here in his room, a foot from his bed, a nightgown beneath her dressing gown, her lovely golden-brown hair spilling over her shoulders, as he'd pictured her.

He cleared his throat. "You must leave, Miss Crabtree," he warned as she moved closer. "It's too dangerous for you to be here."

"Beverly, please. And I'm not ready to leave." She tripped on the hem of her dressing gown and fell into his arms.

Stunned, Jason fell back onto the bed, taking her with him.

"Mm." She nestled against his chest. He breathed in her delicate perfume, a blend of flowers, while his hands brushed over her soft curves free of corsets and petticoats. For a moment, he thought he was in heaven. Then he caught himself and rolled away, putting distance between them.

"Wasn't this what you wanted?" she asked, sounding stricken. "Didn't I lead you to believe that I…"

"You thought I anticipated this? That I expect you to give me your body in lieu of payment for this trip?"

She gasped. "It's horrible when you put it like that."

"It's horrible any way you put it," he said, warily keeping his distance.

"I seem to be mistaken. While I won't become your mistress, I thought we might have one night together. But if you don't want me." Her voice wobbled, and she pushed away from the bed. "I'll go."

He leaped up and grasped her hands, drawing her back down again. "I want you, Beverly. For my wife. That's what I meant by that ill-timed, rash statement."

She shook her head, her heavy locks stirring on her shoulders. "I just want to be with you tonight. We can never marry. I refuse to trap you into a marriage your brother clearly won't agree to. Especially when he hears about my father."

"Let's hope something can be done for your father. That is why we are here, is it not?" He stared at her. "What is this about my brother?"

"The duke came to the Lyon's Den while I was there. After he went in to see Mrs. Dove-Lyon, she came directly to tell my mother that a new suitor was to be found for me." She eyed him. "Then, she introduced me to Mr. Perlew. It is fortunate the gentleman doesn't want me because I didn't like him."

A little tipsy, she made him want to laugh. To make love to her. He averted his gaze as she tugged the hem of her gown over her slender ankles. Her small feet were bare, and he'd give a king's ransom to kiss them, to work his way up. He swallowed. "I see."

He thrust himself off the bed and stalked around the room. It helped him to think not to have her so close. What must be done? He swiveled and came back to her. Deciding not to go down on one knee in his flimsy garment, he sat beside her and raised her hand to his lips. "I love you, sweetheart. I have little to offer you until my twenty-fifth birthday, which is a few years off. But if we can find a way, would you marry me?"

"*Oh, Jason.*" She reached up to trace a finger over his jaw. "Of course, I would, if it were possible, but we both know it's not." She smiled. "You might kiss me, though."

He wasn't at all sure he could stop at one kiss. He'd obviously had one glass too many tonight, and his senses were reeling.

While he was wrestling with his conscience, her arms slipped around him. She pressed her body against his and raised her chin. "Kiss me."

"*Beverly*," he murmured hopelessly and took her mouth.

CHAPTER ELEVEN

J ASON'S HOT KISSES inflamed Beverly's senses. She hugged him and kissed him back.

He eased away, breathing hard, his passionate gaze roaming her face. "You must go now."

"Yes...I should," she murmured. A sensible woman would not be here. Her whole body was aroused and filled with curiosity. She refused to consider it. Edging closer, she reached up and coiled her fingers in his hair, drawing his head back down to hers. "But not yet."

"You are an innocent," he warned, his voice deep and husky. "You're playing with fire."

"I'm sick of being told I'm naïve. Being kept in ignorance hinders one."

Jason chuckled softly. "Does it?" He pulled back, the stern expression in eyes anchoring her attention. "Not if your wedding night is spent with another man. And that could happen, Beverly, if your grandfather has other plans for you."

"So, you didn't mean it when you asked me to marry you?"

His expression softened. "Of course. With every fiber of my being, sweetheart. But there's a very good reason why your grandfather won't accept me."

"I can't believe that. What reason?"

As he explained what happened in Oxford, Beverly's concern and anger on his behalf grew.

"Charles has gone to Oxford. He hopes something can be done to restore my reputation." He shrugged. "I fear it's a waste of time."

"But you are innocent, Jason. It won't matter, for I won't tell Grandpapa anything about it."

"He will have to be told. He's likely to discover it in any event. An article appeared in the Oxford University and City Herald. Better that he hear it from me."

She gazed up at him imploringly. "No! Please don't tell him. It doesn't matter a scrap to me."

"You are a darling," he said, warm admiration in his eyes. "I could obtain a special license. We would have to elope to Gretna Green because, at eighteen, you're underage and cannot marry without parental consent. You'd stay with my mother until we had a home of our own." He frowned and shook his head. "But runaway marriages are not at all the thing, sweetheart. Your parents still suffer the consequences of the elopement." He traced the line of her jaw with a gentle finger. "I don't want that for you. You deserve a wedding performed with propriety, the announcement in the *Morning Post,* and loved ones there to wish us well."

Her grandfather might wield considerable power if he chose, she thought with a tug of panic. Everything was so uncertain. It was fair to assume Jason's brother would cast them out into the cold. Society would then follow suit. His mother might not be so happy to have a daughter-in-law thrust upon her.

While she didn't want a grand wedding, she could not do that to Jason. If what happened tonight was all that ever took place between them, then she would have this memory to cherish.

"I don't want to elope," she insisted. "But I do want to spend these few precious hours with you. I trust you to keep me safe, Jason."

She expected him to argue but was gathered into his arms for another demanding kiss. When his lips nudged hers open, and his tongue slid inside to touch hers, a burning tide of desire flooded over her. Barely able to catch her breath, she murmured against his mouth, her lips quivering at the sensual onslaught. Convinced she'd been right not to fight her feelings, she stroked the silky hair at his nape and boldly tangled her tongue with his, tasting ale and sweet wine. She trembled at the electric effect on her nerve endings, for it seemed to emulate the joining of their bodies. Nothing in her wild imaginings of what lovers did together ever came close to this deep yearning in her heart and the insistent pulse between her thighs.

Jason moaned against her mouth, his hungry kisses, causing her heart to race.

"You should never trust a man," he murmured as his hand somehow found its way into her nightgown to cup her breast.

He toyed with a nipple. The delicious sensation made her shiver. What the future might hold didn't seem to matter. She wanted this now, as much as he did. When his arousal pressed against her thigh, she yearned to touch him but was suddenly shy. Before she could act upon it, he removed his hand from her breast, straightened her nightgown and rose, taking her hand and pulling her up from the bed.

"I shall escort you to your chamber, Miss Crabtree," he said in a strained voice. "And tomorrow, I will ask your grandfather to sanction our marriage, with as clear a conscience as I can manage, while erotic visions of you naked beneath me fill my head."

Beverly, hot and frustrated, managed to giggle.

"Wait here." Jason opened the door and searched the corridor poorly lit by a wall sconce, the candle guttering. "Right, come on," he whispered.

Before she knew it, she stood before her bedchamber door. She turned to say goodnight and found him gone. Lifting the latch, she stepped quietly into the dark room.

Miss George's snoring greeted her.

Beverly picked her way carefully to her bed, tightening her lips on a sigh, and climbed beneath cold sheets, the bedwarmer having long lost any warmth. She lay there remembering him, his kisses, his clean, male smell, and the rasp of soft bristles on his jaw beneath her fingers. She would never be able to sleep now. She almost giggled when she considered that he'd banished all other concerns from her head. But they would return full force tomorrow when she must face her grandfather.

WHILE A STRONG, cool breeze, heavy with the tang of damp earth, whipped the trees about and toyed with the ladies' hats, Jason rode alongside the chaise as the horses drove through the village of Upton Grey.

Jason had been relieved but deeply regretful that he'd resisted making love to Beverly. He had not allowed himself to forget how innocent she was. He'd give his life to keep her safe. At breakfast, they agreed not to send a note to inform her grandfather of their visit, fearing he might refuse to see them.

The road continued on into the countryside. They followed a high stone wall for several miles and came to a pair of carved stone pillars and a set of elaborate gates with *Deane Abbey* emblazoned on them. The carriage passed an empty gatehouse and continued along an arrow-straight gravel drive, tunneled by ancient oaks. The sweep led them through the cropped turf of a fine park, with glimpses of the abbey's gray, stone walls on a slight rise ahead.

The garrulous innkeeper at the Fox and Goose had revealed the abbey's history to Jason when he'd stayed in the taproom after the rest of the guests retired. It had been converted into a home after Henry VIII brought about the Dissolution of the Monasteries and closed down all abbeys, monasteries, and convents.

Jason rode up alongside the chaise for Beverly's reaction. Her face was alight with curiosity beneath her green poke bonnet. She tugged nervously at her gloves. He wanted to offer some reassurance but thought better of it. Any displays of his intentions in front of others would have to wait.

The postboys pulled up the chaise before the mansion, impressive with its twin conical towers soaring into the sky. A short flight of steps led to solid oak doors recessed in a Gothic stone arch, while menacing gargoyles peered from the gutters. Jason thought the building stark. The rows of blank, mullioned windows set in stone embrasures seemed to stare blankly down at them. Shewsbury Park, his family's ducal seat in Leicestershire, had been rebuilt in the last century. Its towering white columns and pale stone walls were far more welcoming. So was the manor house on his more modest estate in Dorset, which he'd inherited from an aunt. Beverly would like it. He could picture her there.

When a groom appeared from the direction of the stables, Jason dismounted and, instructing the man to wait, tossed him the reins. He turned to assist the ladies. Beverly paused to gaze up at the house. "It is just as Mama described," she murmured.

He was escorting the ladies toward the porch when a man's chuckle came from around the corner.

A solidly built gentleman strolled into view dressed in a bronze-colored riding coat, leather breeches, and top boots. An arm was snugly around the trim waist of a much younger lady in a crimson habit.

Standing beside Jason, Beverly gasped.

The 6th Baron Daintith paused on the gravel drive to observe them.

He bent his head and murmured to the woman. She smiled at him and strolled forward, passing them with her head lowered, and ran lightly up the steps to disappear through the doors held open by a liveried footman.

The baron removed his hat to reveal a thick thatch of white hair and strode over to them, a quizzical light in eyes very much like Beverly's. "To what do I owe this visit, granddaughter?"

Beverly hurried forward. "Grandpapa, I am in need of your advice. But please allow me to introduce you to my chaperone, Miss George, and Lord Jason Glazebrook, who kindly escorted us on the journey from London."

"Did he indeed?" The baron cast an assessing look at Jason from beneath shaggy eyebrows as he took his hand in a hearty shake. "How do you do, sir." He turned to welcome Miss George with a nod as she sank into a curtsy. "Let's get out of this infernal cold wind." He turned to the groom. "See to that horse and send the chaise back to the inn."

The baron led them into a lofty salon, the oak floors covered with Turkey rugs, the walls hung with gilt-framed paintings, and tapestries. The embers of a coal fire glowed in the massive stone fireplace. Lord Daintith added coal from the scuttle and prodded the embers into a blaze with a poker, sending smoke swirling up the chimney. He directed them to the sofas and chairs grouped around the fireplace and ordered the footman to bring the decanter of Madeira and send for the tea tray.

"Now." He sat down and crossed muscular legs. "Glazebrook? I knew the old duke. I haven't met your brother, Charles, but I hear good things about him." Not waiting for Jason's response, the baron addressed his granddaughter. "What is it you want from me, Beverly, after all these years?"

After a quick glance at Jason, she leaned forward. "I should like to speak with you alone, Grandpapa."

He cocked his head to one side. "You don't favor your mother.

You are prettier."

Beverly frowned and caught her bottom lip between her teeth.

Jason tamped down a grin. She was inordinately fond of her mother.

A footman and housemaid carried in the tea trays. The footman poured Madeira into crystal glasses for the men, while the maid unloaded the tea service onto the table before the ladies.

"You're putting up at the Fox and Goose?" the baron asked Beverly.

"Yes, Grandpapa."

"What nonsense. You must stay here." He raised a hand to the footman. "John, have their luggage fetched from the inn." He settled back in his chair. "I'm looking forward to a decent game of whist. Sick to death of cribbage."

Jason wondered if they were to meet the lady the duke would have been playing cribbage with. He rather doubted it. Even a man such as the baron did not introduce his mistress to his granddaughter.

After tea, the baron signaled to his footman, who stood again at the door. "John, have the tea tray removed. I believe Miss George would enjoy the knot garden, have her escorted there."

Miss George must have realized Lord Daintith was too much for her to tackle, and stood, leaving the room with a dignified step.

Jason had risen to his feet but was impelled to sit again at the baron's gesture. "I believe you both have something to tell me," Lord Daintith said.

"Grandpapa—"

Beverly was silenced by another of his imperious gestures. "We shall begin with Lord Jason," he said, "Whom I suspect has an interesting proposal to put to me."

Jason had taken the measure of the man at the first sight of him. It appeared he liked to flaunt convention, having installed his mistress here. The knowledge helped Jason decide how to approach him. "I have requested Miss Crabtree's hand in marriage, Lord Daintith," he said bluntly. "I realize I must seek her father's consent, but you shall shortly learn why this is difficult. I would appreciate your support."

A spark appeared in Lord Daintith's eyes. "Would you indeed. And might this be against the duke's wishes?"

"As I've not yet raised it with him, I cannot say, my lord. However, there are other important matters to be dealt with first."

"I am eager to hear of them, sir."

"I believe Miss Crabtree wishes to speak to you about a private matter." Jason rose. "I shall leave you to talk."

The baron frowned, leaving Jason with the fear that he intended to oppose their marriage. But he made no protest as Jason exited the room.

Jason discovered Miss George walking through the great hall with the obvious intention of seeking out Beverly. "I believe I spied what might prove to be a fine old Roman statue in the sunken garden. I'd appreciate your opinion, Miss George. Shall we go and view it?"

Burying an anxious sigh, he offered her his arm, and after a suspicious glance, she allowed him to lead her toward the door.

Chapter Twelve

B EVERLY STRUGGLED TO explain the situation to her grandfather. She didn't know the finer details of her father's troubles, only what her mother had told her. And Mama was inclined to shelter her from the worst. She became flustered and exhausted as he continued to interrupt and ask her questions.

"I'm not sure what you expect me to do for your father," Grandpapa finally said. "It is up to the courts to decide if he is guilty or innocent."

"But it's hard to fight corruption, Grandpapa," she said, her voice shaking. "The Parish constable is rumored to be on the payroll of Lord Paine, who may be connected to a smuggling ring."

He sat forward, his eyes questioning. "Lord Fulbert Paine?"

"Yes."

Her grandfather rose to his feet and proceeded to stalk around the room. It occurred to her that he was seldom still as he swiveled and came back to stand before her chair. "It just so happens that I've had dealings with Paine. I'll advise my legal firm, Minshall, Deaks, and Moffatt, to look into the matter," he said. "I'll send a letter on the mail coach tomorrow."

She dragged in a deep breath, sagging with relief. How tense she'd been. "I am very grateful, Grandpapa."

He sat down again and crossed one leg over the other, tapping a boot with his fingers. "Don't think this means I'll take your mother back into the fold."

"I understand, Grandpapa." Although she wanted to persuade him for her mother's sake, she feared he might change his mind about helping them. She studied her hands in her lap, but when she glanced up again, she found him watching her with a wry smile.

He cocked an eyebrow. "You think me unfair, don't you, lass?"

"Mama's life has not been easy. She was younger than I am when she and my father married. When young and in love, one does not foresee the awful consequences an elopement might cause." How true, that was. If Jason had asked her to elope, she would have gone with him without looking back. "Mama would never have wished an estrangement from you. I suppose she expected you to forgive her."

His beetling brows lowered into a scowl. "Are you judging me, girl?"

"Mama dearly loves my father," Beverly said carefully. "He is a good man."

"He well might be, but Crabtree is an idiot to get himself caught up in this nefarious business. A smart fellow would have dealt with it before it came to this."

"Hard for an honest man, certainly." Beverly raised her chin. "But villains have been working against him."

He nodded approvingly. "You have gumption. More than your mother ever had."

"Mama has gumption," she said, unable to remain silent. "She must have to defy you as she did, Grandpapa."

He nodded approvingly. "You love your mother"

When she caught a glimpse of pain in his eyes, she realized that he, too, had been greatly hurt by this. She wanted to reach out to him, but he was a proud man and would most likely reject it or see it as a means to persuade him. "Perhaps it is time to forgive them," she suggested tentatively.

Grandpapa rose without comment and went to tug the bell pull. When his footman entered, he issued a string of orders, requesting fresh vellum, pens, ink, and wax await him in the library. "Send for the housekeeper," he ordered the footman. "And find Glazebrook. Bring him to the library." His sober, brown gaze rested on Beverly. "My housekeeper will escort you and your chaperone to your chambers. Mrs. Kelly will supply you with anything you need. I shall see you at dinner."

Beverly tamped down the fear at what might take place between Grandpapa and Jason. So much hinged upon it. "Thank you, Grandpapa." On tiptoes, she rested a hand on his broad shoulder and kissed his cheek, breathing in the aromatic smells of tobacco, soap, and leather. "I am glad I came, and not just because you will help us. I've wanted to know you for a long time."

He raised his eyebrows again. "Have I said I would help you and the young man?"

She shook her head. "No...not precisely."

"You are both young. Wiser, surely, to see how things stand in another year or two."

She stared at him in horror. "Oh no! Lord Jason is the only man I wish to marry. And he feels the same about me. You and Grandmama didn't know each other before you married, did you?" From her infancy, her mother had told her all the family stories, how fond her parents were of each other, and how her mother's death had changed him. Her reminiscences always brought tears to Beverly's eyes.

An arm on the mantle, Grandpapa stared into the crackling orange embers, an emotional expression softening his face. "Our marriage was arranged. Love didn't enter into what was seen as a business arrangement. A satisfactory joining of two great families. I was fortunate.

Your grandmother was a wonderful woman." His gray-haired head bowed over the fire as he picked up the poker. He gave the fire a vicious stab, sending sparks flying up the chimney. "Catherine died too young." After a moment's silence, he turned to study her. "She would have loved you, Beverly."

"I would have loved her, Grandpapa. Mama has told me so much about her." Her shy smile implored him. "You knew from the first, didn't you, that your union was right? As I do. You can do so much to help us. *Please*, Grandpapa. Lord Jason is of age and doesn't require his brother's permission to marry, but it would be unendurable if the duke turned against us. A letter from you, urging him to support our marriage, would smooth our way. It would mean so much to Jason."

"So, you expect me to beg for the duke's approval as well, do you?"

Surer of him now, she gave a cheeky grin. "No, but I *am* hopeful."

For a moment, she feared she'd gone too far. But he smiled. "By Jove, Miss, you'll do." He took her arm and gave her a gentle push toward the door. "Don't expect to get 'round me with your feminine wiles. Many women have tried before you. I intend to put your suitor through a rigorous interview before I make up my mind about this marriage."

The housekeeper, Mrs. Kelly, a small, red-haired woman, entered and curtsied before the baron. Given her instructions, she escorted Beverly up the staircase to an opulent bedchamber furnished in teal and gold damask.

"I've ordered hot water to be brought, Miss Crabtree. I'll send a maid to assist you to dress for dinner."

"Thank you, Mrs. Kelly."

"Please ring the bell beside the fireplace if you require anything else."

When the door shut behind her, Beverly stood on the Axminster carpet and gazed appreciatively at the grand chamber, relieved at not having to share it with Miss George.

She crossed the thick carpet to the window and looked down at the well-tended gardens. Beyond them was the stone wall that divided the formal gardens with the south meadow. A fall from it had caused that scar on Mama's knee. Jason and Miss George appeared walking together along a path leading to the house. As always, the sight of him made Beverly's pulse quicken. She raised a hand, but he was talking to her chaperone and didn't look up.

She'd become more confident that Grandpapa would assist in their marriage. He seemed all-powerful. It saddened her to know how much her father had retreated from the man he used to be before the unthinkable happened. That he should have his honor placed in question and be unable to refute it was greatly distressing to him.

But perhaps now, with her grandfather's help, everything would be as it was. And she and Jason would marry!

With a sigh of delight, she spun around and fell back onto the wide, poster bed. Gazing at the swag of sumptuous brocade above, she thought of how much she loved Jason and how wonderful it had been when he'd kissed her.

If only this distressing business which hung over her father's head would end, everyone would be so happy. She plucked at the tassel on a cushion, her mood sobering. Despite discovering her cantankerous grandpapa was not without a kind heart, trepidation made her heart pound when she considered what still might go wrong.

LORD DAINTITH GLARED at Jason. "You tell me you don't have a feather to fly with, and you expect me to welcome you into the family with open arms?"

Seated on the maroon leather sofa in the well-equipped library, Jason swirled the amber liquid in his brandy glass. "But with excellent prospects, sir."

The baron drew on his cigar, then blew out a cloud. "I would prefer Beverly to marry a title. But as her mother defied me and married beneath her, I suppose that is a stretch too far. Your brother is in good health?"

"Excellent health, sir." Jason frowned. Surely the man wasn't querying if he might one day inherit the dukedom? "Charles is soon to marry and intends to set up his nursery."

"No need to climb on your high horse," the baron said mildly. "I merely wished to know how things stood between you and your brother. I can see you're fond of him. So, tell me more about this trust."

When Jason had supplied him with the details of properties and entitlements, Lord Daintith nodded thoughtfully. "I shall furnish Beverly with a handsome dowry. I am unaware of her father's intentions, but I would like him to match it. I'm not hopeful, however. I suspect Crabtree's pockets are not deep."

"That is most generous of you, sir." Jason's relief was palpable.

No furtive dashes to the border, and now, surely, Charles would not oppose the marriage. There was one matter which twisted Jason's gut every time he thought of it. Would the disgrace heaped on him after his expulsion from Oxford reach the baron's ears? The man wouldn't like it. If it had been his daughter, Jason wouldn't like it either, for it showed his character in a very poor light. He had tried to explain the seriousness of it to Beverly, to warn her, but even after hearing it, she'd dismissed it as unimportant.

He couldn't help delighting in the fact that she believed in him. That it never occurred to her he might not be telling the truth or had tied the business up in a rosy package. And there was something he failed to mention. He couldn't bring himself to tell her what he had been doing on the night the boat was tampered with. Still a little ashamed at his part in it, he groaned inwardly. Dare he hope Charles had managed to bring about a miracle?

"I've written to my lawyers," the baron said, drawing him back. "We'll see if something might be done for Crabtree." He swilled a mouthful of brandy before swallowing it. "No reason why you and my granddaughter cannot tie the knot here in Deane Abbey chapel."

"We would be honored, sir." Jason shoved his uneasy thoughts away. "But Beverly will want her parents to come."

Daintith nodded. "Naturally. I'm sure they will attend."

Jason was inclined to agree. Although he doubted the baron's invitation would be couched in terms of a reconciliation, he suspected the Crabtrees were unlikely to oppose such an advantageous arrangement.

It must have been a terrible blow to a man like Daintith when his daughter defied him and ran off. And Crabtree, a mere solicitor, who hailed from the gentry. Beverly's grandfather seemed unlikely to forgive past hurts. Was he being amenable now because he was lonely and regretted the loss of his family? Or did he relish the opportunity to rub Crabtree's nose in what he considered the man's incompetence? He might even have lingering doubts as to his son-in-law's honesty. Jason didn't much care what his reason was, as long as the outcome was successful, and he and Beverly could marry.

He shook Daintith's strong hand and quit the room, grasping his approval like a rope thrown to a sailor in the sea surrounded by sharks.

CHAPTER THIRTEEN

T HERE WERE FOUR to dinner. Miss George had been invited, but the lady they had seen with her grandfather when they first arrived did not attend. After an elaborate array of courses, consisting of fresh trout, venison, baked chicken, and fresh vegetables from the estate, served in delicious sauces, the two footmen removed the covers and served a syllabub, cheese, fruit, and a plate of nuts.

A lively discussion took place on the benefits of gas lamps now lighting the streets in St. Margaret's Westminster and how London would look in December when more areas would be lit. As they employed the nutcracker to the walnuts, Jason and her grandfather argued about what horse would win the Thousand Guineas Stakes at Newmarket. Beverly was always amused at how heated these discussions became. She remembered her father and brother in happier times.

No agreement had been reached as Miss George and Beverly left the men to their port and cigars. But they did not tarry long. Jason and her grandfather chuckling over some antidote, and apparently on good terms, soon joined them in the salon where a card table had been set up.

The cards were dealt as the footman, John, served brandy and Madeira, then with a bow, left the room. Her grandfather played cards with the same intensity with which he seemed to do everything. He won the final rubber, tossed back the last of his brandy, and went to the sideboard for the decanter. "Care for a game of billiards?" he asked Jason as he replenished their glasses.

"Most agreeable, thank you, sir." Jason's gaze found Beverly's. They would have little opportunity to be alone tonight.

The card table was removed, and the silver tea service brought in. "You may pour, my dear," her grandfather said from his chair opposite the sofa. "A ride before breakfast?"

"I didn't bring riding clothes, Grandpapa." Beverly opened the tea caddie and spooned the leaves into the warmed teapot. She added hot water. "We must leave for London quite early. Mama could have returned from Horsham, and I don't want her to worry."

"Ah. Shame. The bridle trails here are excellent, and I did want to show you more of the estate. Next time then."

"I look forward to it," Beverly said ruefully.

She would enjoy it. She had slipped into the gallery before coming down to dinner and viewed the oil paintings of her ancestors. There were a few men and women from the past who had brown eyes similar to hers and Grandpapa's, and it made her feel more a part of the Daintiths. It also made her aware of the importance of family and what she had been missing.

When the dishes were removed, the men left the room to play billiards. Beverly was tired, but she didn't want to retire just yet. She'd visited the library and discovered a riveting book of drawings and surreptitiously studied each page, glad of its plain cover.

Miss George, seated in an armchair, employed her needle to her sampler with deft stitches. She'd said little since they'd come to the abbey and was silent during dinner. Perhaps she felt awkward about the difference in their social standing, but Beverly couldn't quite believe it. Miss George seemed indomitable.

She was startled and quickly closed the book when her chaperone suddenly addressed her. "It has been a pleasant journey, and I am pleased for you and Lord Jason if something comes of it." She snipped a thread with her scissors. "But I confess, I am eager to return to London."

"Because of Mr. Perlew?" Beverly ventured. She tucked the book under a cushion while pushing away visions of naked men and women cavorting in extraordinary poses.

"No. I don't imagine he's given me another thought. I must seek new employment."

"Oh. Of course." Beverly suffered a stab of guilt. Her thoughts had been filled with her own concerns. Poor Miss George, her future did look uncertain. Beverly hoped there might be something she could do to help her, but until she was married, she was powerless.

A half-hour later, Jason entered the room. "Would you ladies care for a stroll on the terrace before you retire? The wind has died down, and it's pleasant out."

"What a nice idea." Beverly rose as her fatigue fell away.

Jason took up her Norwich shawl and arranged it over her shoulders. "Miss George?"

"I believe I shall retire," she said unexpectedly as she put away her embroidery. "It's been a long day, and I'm a little tired."

"My goodness," Beverly said to Jason when they stepped out into the fragrant night air. "I do hope Miss George is not too exhausted."

"That was most unlike her." He slipped an arm around her waist. "But I am not about to complain."

She turned within his arm to gaze up into his face. In the moonlight, his eyes were warm and inviting. "Still, we must be discreet."

He sighed. "To please your chaperone?"

"She has placed her trust in us."

"Clever, Miss George," Jason said wryly. He dropped his arm and moved to the banister rail.

She joined him and stood observing the flickering shadows cast over the gardens by the braziers.

He leaned his back against the rail, glancing up at the windows above them. "I imagine I have little hope of a goodnight kiss then. Your zealous chaperone is probably looking down at us at this moment."

Beverly giggled. "Then, it is an excellent opportunity to talk. We shan't be able to on the way back to London. There is so much I want to know about your family."

"Mm. Where shall I begin?"

"I would like to hear about your mother and your childhood, but first, tell me about your brother. I know he's an honorable man because Miss George told me so."

"How did she come to know that?"

"She read about him in the *Morning Post*."

"Ah."

Charles was of a similar height to Jason but of a bigger stature. "I thought your brother strong and athletic when I saw him at the Lyon's Den."

Jason nodded. "We rode with the Quorn in Leicestershire when we were younger. The hunting is pretty wild there, and you throw your heart over the fences. But Charles is keen on many sports— racing, fencing, sparing at Jackson's boxing salon…"

She smiled. "You are fond of him."

"Yes, we were always close." He rubbed his jaw. "Charles hasn't been quite himself for a while. I guess my older brother Michael's death left a large hole in our hearts, and then father dying a year ago. Perhaps this summer after Charles returns to Shewsbury Park, he'll feel more comfortable. He takes a great interest in the running of the estate. And the sheep."

"Sheep?"

"It's sheep country." Jason grinned. "Charles is to marry later this year. I imagine that will bring about change. You'll like him."

"Will he like me?"

He took her in his arms and held her close, nuzzling her neck. "Of course, he will," he murmured, his warm breath on her skin, making her tremble. "What's not to like?"

With a glance at the lighted room behind him, she quickly kissed him, then stepped out of his arms, fighting the impulse to remain. "Shall I meet your mother when in London?"

"I'm not sure. My mother seldom comes to London since Father died. She is much involved in the parish and county affairs. She plans to move into the dower house at Shewsbury Park when Charles brings his bride home."

"She sounds...formidable."

"Mother?" He smiled. "She is a determined lady, but never un-kind."

"Oh, I'm glad."

He stroked her arms. "Of course, my mother will attend our wed-ding. I know she will come to love you."

While she wasn't confident, she did hope his family would like her. Nothing Jason had told her allayed her fears, however. If her father should go to prison... A chill crept down her spine.

"You're trembling, my sweet," Jason drew her back into his arms. "Are you cold?"

At a cough, they broke apart.

Her grandfather stood in the doorway, the smoke from a cigar in his long fingers drifting out into the night. "Time for you two lovebirds to retire to your separate chambers."

"Yes, it grows late." Jason tucked Beverly's arm into the crook of his and led her inside. "A long journey awaits us tomorrow."

"Quite." Her grandfather's eyes twinkled as she passed him.

THE NEXT DAY dawned fine, although a looming, dark cloud bank threatened on the horizon. Jason accompanied the chaise on Centaur, the horse fresh and eager for a run. The rain held off, and the roads were excellent. They made good time. As the sun climbed higher in the sky, he rode on ahead to secure luncheon at the coaching inn.

Some hours later, they approached the inn where Charles's horses were stabled.

Drops of rain struck his hat. He glanced uneasily at the sky as he dismounted in the inn yard.

While he waited for the innkeeper to finish dealing with another couple, Jason's thoughts returned to their departure. Lord Daintith had offered him some last-minute advice. "When you meet Crabtree, might be prudent not to mention you'd sought my help in his affairs," he'd said, standing in the carriageway as they waited for the ladies to come down. "A proud man, he won't appreciate my interference, and I doubt he'd welcome a family reunion after all this time. I have advised my lawyers to be discreet." He gave a wry smile. "Not everything to do with this family rift can be laid at my door." He sighed. "But I must admit, I have been wrong on occasion."

Jason hoped he didn't look too surprised at Daintith's confession. He offered his hand. "I appreciate the advice."

The baron seized his hand in a firm grip and shook it. "Just smoothing the way, Glazebrook. I merely want to see my investment come to fruition."

As Jason followed the chaise down the carriageway, he'd glanced back. The baron still stood on the drive. The pretty lady who had not been sighted again during their stay appeared at the door.

The baron might flout some of society's rules, Jason thought, but he would value a gentleman's code of honor. Daintith would certainly withdraw his support if he learned of that shameful business at Oxford.

It approached dusk when they finally reached the outskirts of London the next day and pulled up in Half Moon Street.

As he helped the ladies alight, the door opened, and lamplight shone out. A maid hurried onto the porch.

Jason paid the postboys, who were unloading and piling the luggage in the hall. Miss George said goodbye to him and disappeared up the stairs.

After Beverly spoke to the maid, she hurried back down the path to where he held Centaur's rein. "My mother has returned, but she is resting. I must go to her."

"I'll call tomorrow, my love." Jason settled his hat on his head and swung up into the saddle.

"Tomorrow," Beverly called.

He watched her enter the house and then gently nudged his tired horse's flanks. As he rode home, Jason steeled himself for what lay ahead. Would Charles have good news for him? Never had it been so important. Not only his reputation but his future happiness hinged on it. It went against his sense of honor to withhold his past from the baron, but whatever way he painted the affair, he wouldn't come out smelling like a rose. However, he fully intended to reveal it before he and Beverly were wed, whatever news Charles had for him.

After stabling his horse and giving unnecessary instructions to the zealous groom, Jason patted Centaur's rump and left, making his way to the house. The butler informed him that the duke planned to attend the Montgomerys' ball later in the evening. He'd left word he wished to see Jason in the library as soon as he came in.

Jason resisted the inclination to rush in. "Tell my brother I'll join him as soon as I've washed and changed, Grove. And ask the kitchen staff to rustle up a meal for me. A cold collation will do."

Jason raced up the stairs, feeling a bit unsteady as if his whole life was held in the balance. And how would Charles react to what Jason was about to tell him?

Chapter Fourteen

EVERLY HURRIED INSIDE. Cousin Granville sat in the parlor with two gentlemen. When they rose to their feet, she went in to greet them, tamping down her eagerness to see her mother. "Welcome home, Cousin Granville. Did you have an enjoyable sojourn?"

"We did, thank you. We're a little fatigued, as we've only just arrived back in good old London. But how grown you are, Beverly." Coming forward, a smile in his weary blue eyes, he took her hands and introduced her to the two older gentlemen. "What a pity we won't see more of you. Your mother has told me you leave for Horsham on the stage tomorrow."

"Oh, I didn't know. I've been visiting Grandpapa in Upton Grey. Please excuse me. I must go up to her."

Shocked by the news, Beverly ran upstairs. She opened the door to her mother's bedchamber. Mama lay on the bed with a cloth over her eyes. She pulled it off and sat up. "Beverly!"

Beverly hurried to sit beside her on the bed. "Mama, I'm sorry you've been so worried. I did leave a note, but I had no idea how things would turn out. I have so much to tell you."

"I could not believe that you went to see your grandfather without asking my consent. You know how things stand between us. How could you? What will your father say? I should be so cross, but right at this moment, I am too exhausted and relieved to see you safe."

She laid her head back on the pillow and closed her eyes. "Please do hurry and explain. I confess all this has made me nauseous." Mama opened her eyes again. "We cannot remain here now that Cousin Granville has returned. And his companions will want the best rooms. Most vexing. But we must go in any event. Unless something happens, your father will be hauled up before the judge. I have been able to book two seats on the stagecoach, which leaves in the morning."

"Oh, no! But Mama, Lord Jason is calling tomorrow. He has asked me to marry him."

"It won't do a bit of good, Beverly. You will not marry Lord Jason Glazebrook."

Beverly gasped. "But Grandpapa has given us his blessing."

Her mother's mouth tightened.

"You wanted me to marry Lord Jason, Mama. You and Mrs. Dove-Lyon plotted..."

Her mother flushed. "Mrs. Dove-Lyon wishes the best for you, Beverly. She has discovered an unsavory incident concerning Lord Jason. Your father will not accept him."

"Lord Jason explained what happened at Oxford. It isn't true. He's innocent, Mama!"

Her mother firmed her lips. "Nevertheless, Mrs. Dove-Lyon has another gentleman in mind. He is wealthy and comes from an excellent family."

"Mama... no! I love Lord Jason."

"But, Beverly...my dear." Agitated, her mother plucked at the shawl over her shoulders. "A young woman cannot always choose who she marries. Without wisdom and guidance, she might well come to regret it."

Beverly doubted Mama had ever regretted marrying Papa, but she didn't say so; she hated to see her so distressed. "Lord Jason has integrity. He would never lie to me," she said in a gentler voice. "And he loves me."

"I came to realize what a bad choice it would be for you because the duke is so fervently against the marriage. He came to the Lyon's Den to put a stop to it." She sighed. "As Lord Jason has not the means to support you, you'd be dependent upon his brother's charity. I'm fully aware of how destructive bad blood within a family can be."

"I know, but Lord Jason feels sure that..."

Her mother held up her hand. "Enough! We will send a note to Lord Jason to advise him of our decision. And thank him, of course, for his assistance, which was good of him. I trust...although..." She cast another anxious glance at Beverly. "I hope Miss George performed her duties well?"

"She was most zealous in her attentions." Recalling the night she spent with Jason, Beverly blushed. Fortunately, her mother was too distracted to notice.

"Well, that is good news, at least! But all this is making my megrim worse! And we must pack for the long, tedious coach trip tomorrow."

"But what about Miss George?" Beverly asked. "We can't just cast her out!"

"Well, of course, we cannot. Did you think I would be so cruel? Granville has kindly agreed to allow her to remain until she has another position.

"Where is that maid?" Mama said fretfully. "I rang for her ten minutes ago."

Her heart aching, Beverly could do nothing but retire to her bedroom and have Daisy pack for Horsham. She took out Jason's handkerchief to wipe away her tears. She so hated weakness, but all her hopes and dreams, so rosy only a short time ago, seemed to have turned to ashes. Unless she held on to the hope that her grandfather would come to her aid, despite her good sense telling her it was unlikely. Jason would not give up, she was sure, but she could not turn him against his brother. He was so fond of him; she must be strong.

CHARLES SAT BACK in his desk chair and surveyed him. "I wish I had better news," he said, striking a knife into Jason's heart. "Bernard Forbush has gone to live in Italy. Basil Wheelwright is very ill. On his deathbed, it's said. I have asked the chaplain to visit him."

Jason sank into a chair. "I'd best tell you where I've been."

"I expect it to be most interesting," Charles said wryly.

A half-hour later, Jason, having shared the lavish meal Cook sent up with Charles, had resorted to drinking brandy.

"You've done the best you could, Jason," Charles said, eating the last of the cheese. "I'm impressed, I must say. As you have not faltered in your devotion to Miss Crabtree, I trust your good sense not to risk your future by marrying the wrong woman. I certainly cannot withhold my blessing. I offer it wholeheartedly."

"Thank you, Charles." Despite the uncertainty, Jason was pleased. "If we are able to marry, it's my hope that you will stand up as my best man."

Charles nodded with a smile. "I am honored. I hope to have good news soon concerning the trust."

"A lot appears to stand in our way," Jason said. "I will write to Baron Daintith and explain the situation. And Crabtree, too, of course."

Charles pushed back his chair and stood. "I must change for the ball. Get a good night's sleep. Things might look brighter in the morning."

"Or a good deal gloomier," Jason said, following him out of the library.

CHAPTER FIFTEEN

B Y MORNING, BEVERLY'S mother still had not changed her mind. As they donned their hats before the mirror, their luggage piled in the hall awaiting the arrival of the hackney, a knock came on the front door. Daisy rushed to open it.

Mr. Perlew stood on the doorstep, hat in hand. His eyes widened, and he cleared his throat. "Good day, Mrs. Crabtree, Miss Crabtree." He turned the hat around and around by its brim.

"Mr. Perlew, how surprising to see you, especially at the crack of dawn," her mother said crisply.

She had not forgiven him for rejecting Beverly. Mama had spoken of it over breakfast. In her opinion, the man lacked both taste and good sense, and how glad was she that Beverly wasn't to marry him.

"Have you come to see Miss George, sir?" Beverly asked, attempting to ease the poor man's discomfort.

"Ah, yes, I do apologize. Calling this early is not the thing at all. But I did hope to speak to Miss George for a moment. I am on my way to the country for a few days. But I see you are about to embark on a journey as well. Is Miss George…?"

"No, she does not accompany us." Beverly turned to the maid, who stood at the front door. "Daisy, will you tell Miss George, Mr. Perlew is here to see her?"

At that moment, the hackney pulled up outside in the street. As their goodbyes had been said to Cousin Granville and Miss George, whom Beverly had warmly wished well, they nodded to Mr. Perlew and left the house.

They settled themselves in the hackney. "How odd that a stickler for convention like Mr. Perlew would call so early. I wonder if he intends to marry Miss George?" Beverly asked idly, in an effort to distract herself from the heartache which plagued her.

Mama was fussing with her parcels. "If so, I pity her."

"I do hope so. Better, surely, than taking another position. She wishes to have children."

Mama looked up from examining a parcel wrapped in brown paper. "MaryAnne George? She seems so, I don't know, old-maidish. I can't imagine. Well, never mind. If that is the case, then I am happy for her."

Beverly took one last look back at the house as the hackney took them to Blossom's Inn, where they were to board the stagecoach for Brighton. The most wonderful period of her life was over. So much had happened in such a short time. Grief brought tears to her eyes, and she slumped on the squab. She had asked Daisy to add her letter to Jason, explaining all, to the one her mother had written to him. The kitchen boy was to deliver them this morning. What would Jason make of the news? Would he come after her? Her father would only turn him away. If by some miracle, Grandpapa succeeded in his efforts to clear her father's name, would it change Papa's mind about their marriage? She feared it wouldn't. Not unless the duke returned from Oxford with news that would exonerate Jason. And now, to make matters worse, the loathsome Mrs. Dove-Lyon had advised her mother of a new suitor. She was not about to let them go when there was more money to be made. The way forward suddenly seemed blocked by a solid brick wall impossible to climb. *You throw your heart over,* Jason had said when speaking of riding to hounds. If there was something she could do, no matter how bold, she would throw her heart over and take a chance. But what?

THE TWO LETTERS, one from Mrs. Crabtree and one from Beverly, were delivered to Jason as he ate a late breakfast. He pushed his plate away when their contents made his stomach clench. Charles was still asleep, not having returned home much before dawn. Jason drank the last of his coffee and left the table.

Beverly had written that her mother was taking her home to Horsham, and things looked very bad indeed for her father. The ink was slightly smudged where she'd written that he must forget her because his family would never accept her. He didn't care a jot for that. But Crabtree would likely reject his suit. And now a new suitor had presented himself at the Lyon's Den.

Jason left the breakfast room and made his way upstairs. Anger bubbled up inside him at the way the university had failed to investigate fully the claim against him. But mostly, his rage was centered on Mrs. Dove-Lyon. He stalked up and down in need of his brother's opinion and waited for Charles to appear.

Eventually, the door opened. "I can't decide. Was it your gnashing of teeth that woke me? Or your stomping up and down the hall?" Charles asked, yawning as he emerged from his bedchamber, tying the sash of his banyan worn over his shirt and riding breeches. He ran a hand over his freshly shaven jaw. "It was fortunate that Feeley didn't cut me. Is this angst the result of some new development?"

"I'll tell you while you eat," Jason said grimly.

"If it cannot wait. You obviously have no sympathy for my digestion," Charles observed as he headed downstairs.

By the time Charles put away a rasher of bacon, sausage, kidneys, eggs, and several slices of toast and was on his third cup of coffee, the letters had been produced, read, and discussed at length.

"What makes you so sure that Crabtree is innocent of the charges?" Charles asked.

"In the past, Lord Daintith has crossed paths with this Lord Paine, who plans to get rid of Crabtree and become magistrate himself. Says Paine is a crook. He has directed his lawyers to hire Bow Street Runners to investigate the man." Jason frowned. "That will take time."

"The man's insidious, and so far, the authorities haven't been able to prove any wrongdoing. But he's arrogant, and that might trip him up when he seeks to widen his criminal enterprises."

"He might never be brought to justice," Jason said despondently. "All I know is the life I hoped for has gone." Jason stared moodily into space, as his vision of Beverly smiling at him over breakfast faded.

"Not yet it hasn't. We will work to change what we can," Charles said. "And trust Daintith to do the rest. I remain hopeful."

"And what can we change exactly?"

"I've heard from Clegg. He has examined the trust, which appears not to be as watertight as I expected. Perhaps Father planned it that way. I'd like to get that weasel Basil Wheelwright's deathbed confession, though," Charles added thoughtfully.

Jason raised his eyebrows. "Shall I go and choke it out of him?"

"Let the chaplain manage it in a less violent manner. He can appeal to Basil's fear of the Almighty. We'll hear from him in a day or so."

"I'm going to ride down to Horsham. I must see Beverly. She is upset."

"There's no point in rushing down there until you stand on firmer ground. Right now, come for a ride in Hyde Park. It will clear your head of the brandy fumes, which are affecting your thinking. I noticed the empty decanter."

"More than my usual." Jason rubbed his forehead. "If Beverly and I marry, I don't intend to touch another drop of brandy."

"Nonsense, of course you will. Necessary, I imagine, when pacing the floor while your wife gives birth."

"You might face parenthood before I do," Jason said, thinking it was time to discuss Charles's problems instead of his.

Charles nodded. "I've been invited to visit Dountry Park in Cumbria in April to meet Lady Cornelia. When the dreaded measles should no longer be a threat."

"You'd best brush up on your poetry then. I've heard she is a blue-stocking. Favors the bards," Jason said, attempting to inject some humor into the situation. His brother was as far from a poet as the sun was from the moon.

Charles raked an agitated hand through his hair and made a noise somewhere between a moan and a growl. "I hope she doesn't anticipate flowery verses."

Jason cast a quick look at him. "Come on. You need this exercise more than I do."

TWO DAYS LATER, Charles, holding a letter, walked into Jason's bedchamber, where his valet was brushing his coat. "We have it," he said with a grin.

"I don't believe it!" Jason whirled around. He snatched the paper from Charles's fingers and perused it hungrily. Jason chortled. "My God! Basil has confessed! I'm off to Horsham."

"I've asked the chancellor to request a retraction from the University Press. Best wait until you have it in your hands."

Jason scowled. "One of Dove-Lyon's clients could be haring down to Horsham as we speak, ready to fall in love with Beverly."

Charles laid a heavy hand on his shoulder. "Does Beverly love you?"

"Yes, but…"

"Have faith in the girl."

CHAPTER SIXTEEN

BEVERLY SAT WITH her arms around her knees on the grassy bank beside the river flowing through her father's land. She'd fed all the bread Cook had given her to the ducks, and they'd wandered off, back to the water. Through the trees, their manor house overlooked the river from a slight rise, a rambling but handsome building of apricot brick with white-painted shutters. A flowering creeper grew over one wall.

Home had always been her refuge. A place to come back to rest. But it failed her now. She couldn't bear to be in the house. Her father looked so pale, he was almost ghostly, and it frightened her. When Mama fussed around him, he waved her away. No reprieve had been forthcoming. The Assizes sat at the end of the week, and her father would appear before the judge. Mama had advised Mrs. Dove-Lyon of their return but refused to leave Papa in his hour of need. Mrs. Dove-Lyon's reply came only a few days later to say the gentleman was happy to await their return to London.

It was all moving too fast. Beverly had placed a great deal of faith in her grandfather, but perhaps even he could do little to help them. She'd heard nothing from Jason. He must have taken her advice to forget her.

Sighing, she picked up Friday, a black and white kitten, and the one she liked best from the newest litter and walked back to the house. The loose strings of her bonnet swung against her neck, and she wore her plainest morning gown of faded pink with a grass stain near the knee, her fingers grubby from feeding the ducks.

As she crossed from the rose arbor to the front door, a coach rattled down the driveway. Beverly stood rooted to the spot, the kitten wriggling in her arms. The breeze seized her straw hat and flung it into the azaleas. She brushed away a ringlet threatening to blind her and watched as the coach pulled up. The groom opened the door and jumped out but had no time to put down the steps before Jason leaped out.

He reached her quickly and beamed at her, love in his eyes. "Beverly!"

"Jason..." The kitten managed its escape, leaping from her loosened grasp. Jason laughed and quickly recaptured the animal. He held the small, writhing body out to her. "Have you heard the news about your father?"

She took it and cradled it against her bodice, where her heart fluttered. "No. What news?"

"Then we must be the bearers of it. A most pleasant task, I must say." His eyes roamed her face. "Are you well? I've missed you, sweetheart."

She drew in a deep breath. "Oh, I have missed you, too, Jason, so very much."

"My darling, I must tell you..."

"Am I to meet the young lady, Jason?" The Duke of Shewsbury, who had alighted in a more dignified manner, approached them.

"Beverly, Miss Crabtree, allow me to introduce you to my brother, Charles, Duke of Shewsbury," Jason said formally.

"Your Grace," Painfully aware of her disheveled appearance, Beverly sank into a curtsey while the kitten stabbed her chest with its tiny claws.

The duke's blue eyes smiled down at her. How very like Jason he was. Older and broader, but just as handsome. "It's good to meet you, at last, Miss Crabtree. My brother has told me much about you."

Beverly flushed and glanced at Jason. "Please, tell me about my father," she pleaded.

"We should discuss it in Mr. Crabtree's presence," Jason said, a knowing smile on his face.

Her mother, her face crimson, stood in the hall. "Your Grace, Lord Jason, please do come into the drawing room. You'll be in need of a libation after your journey. I shall send for Mr. Crabtree." She looked pained. "I believe he is in the glass house."

While the gentlemen were shown into the drawing room, Beverly excused herself and took the kitten down to the kitchen where word had spread. Cook was in a dither ordering the scullery and kitchen maids about.

Beverly darted upstairs to change and tie a ribbon around her hair. When she came down, her father had been found, and the three men were conversing.

Mama rushed into the room. "A letter has come for you, Mr. Crabtree."

"It appears the news has arrived," Jason said. "It travels slowly in these parts. Please do read it, sir."

Apologizing, her father rose to open and read the missive. A moment later, he looked up, shocked. "It seems my name has been cleared. Lord Paine has been arrested."

"We left London as soon as we had word." Jason smiled at her.

As he spoke, the knocker sounded on the front door. A maid came to fetch Beverly's father.

"Your grandfather's lawyers had some success," Jason said when they were left alone with Charles. "Bow Street Runners engaged by the solicitors exposed some of Lord Paine's disreputable dealings in the city. Found him red-handed at the docks with a gang of smugglers about to load Paine's stolen goods. He resides in Newgate at present."

"It's to be hoped that will keep him in prison, at least until more damning evidence is found. Some members of the gang may confess to save their own hides. He has blood on his hands."

"A clerk from the magistrate's court just called. The parish constable has been arrested." Her father stepped into the room with a big smile. "It is the most unexpected and welcome news." He kissed her mother's cheek and then came to sit down. "I suspect this is your doing, Your Grace and Lord Jason. I must thank you both. I am forever in your debt."

"No, sir. We are merely the bearers of good tidings," Charles said. "Your father-in-law is the one to thank."

"Eh?" Her father's eyes widened in astonishment. "Daintith? What has the baron to do with this?"

Her mother had decided it was better not to tell him about Beverly's trip to Upton Grey. Beverly hurried over to his chair. "I must tell you, Papa, that I went to see Grandpapa with Lord Jason."

"To Deane Abbey?" He raised an eyebrow and turned to look at Jason. "Now, there's a story I look forward to hearing." He picked up his wine glass and downed the contents.

Jason leaned forward. "I should like to speak to you privately, sir."

Charles stood. "Miss Crabtree, would you kindly show me the grounds? Your gardeners have done splendid work here."

Jason winked at Beverly as she took the duke's proffered arm. He seemed so sure. Had there been word? If only he had told her. She was on tenterhooks! Surely her father wouldn't refuse Jason now? She wished she could be sure. This affair had made her father an even harsher critic of what he considered unethical behavior.

"I shall take you to my favorite place, Your Grace, by the river."

"I am eagerness itself."

As they left the room, her mother hovered in the hall with Beverly's best bonnet and handed it to her. "I do hope you and Lord Jason can stay to dinner, Your Grace."

"We should be delighted, Mrs. Crabtree."

Heated flooded Mama's face. "If you'll excuse me, I must instruct Cook."

Beverly led him down the steps into the sunshine. "We'll hear talk of this in the kitchen for a month of Sundays," she confessed.

Charles laughed.

When they reached the river, Charles turned to her. "Did Jason tell you his name has been cleared?"

"No!" Relief flooded through her. "He might have told me."

Charles laughed. "He was so happy to see you. He really didn't get the chance. I won't supply you the details, however. He'll wish to tell you himself."

"I'd begun to fear we'd never see each other again." She choked and pulled Jason's freshly laundered handkerchief from her pocket.

"Some things are meant to be." Charles eyed the crest in the corner and smiled. "A trifle precipitate, but welcome to the family, Beverly."

She smiled shyly. "Thank you, Your Grace."

They turned as a large duck made a clumsy landing on the river and sent up a wide spray, wetting the duke's boots and the hem of her dress. The duke retreated to a safe distance.

"That's Gaffey," she said, horrified and embarrassed. "He's sweet but a little too fond of his food."

"I suspect you aren't fattening him up for Christmas," the duke said with a laugh.

"Oh, no," she gasped. "Not Gaffey!"

JASON WALKED FROM the trees into the sunshine. He spied Beverly and his brother by the river.

"I have become decidedly de trop," Charles said as Jason joined them. "I gather by the look on your face, all went well. My felicitations."

"Yes, very well, thank you, Charles."

After his brother walked away, Jason shook his head with a rueful grin. "That's Charles for you, always trying to steal my thunder."

He drew her into his arms and kissed her. "I've been thinking of doing that all the way here," he said when he finally drew away.

His kisses made her breathless, his lips warm and soft. She smiled, her heart pounding. "Papa has consented to our marriage? Oh, Jason. I can hardly believe it!"

"Believe it, my love."

She clung onto him, her knees unsteady. "Tell me what happened in Oxford."

"The chaplain obtained a signed confession from one of the men who accused me," he said. "Basil Wheelwright admitted that a lark he and Bernard Forbush concocted, turned into something far more serious when the bowman, Anthony Fordham, was knocked unconscious when he fell into the water and almost drowned. When I overheard them speaking of it, they decided to lay the blame on me. Basil has since passed away."

She gazed lovingly up at him. "It's miraculous how it's all turned out. Papa, too."

"Thanks to Lord Daintith."

"Grandpapa is wonderful! I'm so happy I've finally got to know him and to learn more about my family."

"He is quite an extraordinary gentleman. I'm pleased to have met him."

"Did Papa agree to have the wedding held at Deane Abbey?" she asked.

"I thought it might be better if we broach that subject together."

"I pray he does. It will help to put an end to the family feud. But I don't care where we marry. I love you so much, Jason. I just want to be with you."

"I feel the same, darling." He pressed a kiss to her palm. "I feared Mrs. Dove-Lyon would have sent some suitor down here to claim you."

She shook her head at him. "As if I would look at another man."

"My good friend, Will Denning, tells me Mr. Perlew came to the Lyon's Den to advise Mrs. Dove-Lyon that he wouldn't require her services. He is to marry Miss George."

"Oh, I am so pleased for her," Beverly cried. "I am sure they will suit very well."

"Mm. Few surprises there." He held her close. "Not a passionate marriage, I'll wager. Apparently, there was a heated argument between him and Mrs. Dove-Lyon on the matter of fees. She had a bouncer remove Perlew from the premises."

"Oh, my goodness." Beverly gave a peal of laughter.

An arm around her waist, they gazed out over the river. "We could be in our house sooner than I thought. Charles is hopeful of breaking the trust."

"Tell me all about the property. I want to know every detail."

"There's excellent woodland and good pastures," he began as they turned to walk back to the house. "And the manor house, although not grand, is comfortable."

EPILOGUE

"COME BACK TO bed, sweetheart."

Beverly turned from the hotel window. She had been watching a golden eagle soar and dip over the beautiful Scottish loch where they were honeymooning. "Wasn't the wedding perfect?" she asked again as she slipped into the bed beside him and leaned her head against his chest, his arms enclosing her. "The chapel was glorious, wasn't it? All marble and gold with urns of white flowers everywhere. I'll never forget walking down the aisle on Papa's arm, with you so handsome, standing at the altar with Charles."

She smiled as she recalled how Grandpapa nodded his approval, seated in the pew beside her mother, her mother-in-law, her sister, Anabel, all the way from Wales, with her husband and their children, and Granville; the rest of the pews filled with friends and relatives. Then the sumptuous wedding breakfast which followed the signing of the register, and finally, the orchestra playing Mozart in the ballroom as she and Jason danced a waltz.

"You were the most beautiful bride in all of England." Jason kissed the sensitive hollow beneath her ear.

She leaned into him, breathing in his scent. "It was wonderful to see Mama and Grandpapa on good terms again." She traced her fingers through the curls of dark hair on his chest, circling a dark brown nipple. "Grandpapa and Papa were polite to each other, but I doubt they will ever be close." Although very different men, her father was eternally grateful to her grandfather. "It doesn't matter if they're not so close," she said. "For Mama is happy."

"*Mm.*" Jason slowly and provocatively eased her nightgown up over her legs.

"And I thought your mother charming."

"I don't wish to speak of my mother now, Beverly."

She felt his arousal, and her pulse quickened. "And next week, we move into our home. I shall be very busy."

"I intend to keep you very busy," he said.

Her nightgown was tossed onto a chair, and Jason's long body covered hers. His heated look inflamed her, driving a surge of passionate need through her.

"I love you." She stroked the satiny skin on his broad shoulders and back. How thrilling a man's body was.

"I adore you, my love." Jason kissed her and ran a hand over the curve of her hip and belly to the vee of hair below. She shivered slightly. "Are you cold, sweetheart?"

"No," she murmured. "Don't stop, Jason."

"Shall I pull up the bedcover?"

She shook her head. "I like to look at my handsome husband."

"Do you, my temptress?" He kissed her mouth, then nibbled and kissed his way down her to her breasts.

Jason gently cupped her breasts and teased first one nipple, then the other with his tongue. Grabbing fistfuls of the sheet, she moaned, arching her hips in invitation. She ached for him. She would never tire of making love to him. "*Now*, Jason."

"You have beautiful legs, my love," he murmured huskily. Ignoring her demands, he gently held her foot in his hand and kissed her toes, making her giggle, then moved up her leg to press his lips to the inside of her knee.

When Jason's kisses reached her inner thigh, she wriggled and mewed with pleasure as he found that special place. His clever fingers and his mouth taunted her, stirring a fierce, demanding need. *"Oh... please."* Her fingers raked his hair, then gripped his shoulders. Exquisite sensations built and became almost unbearable, then shattered and sent her spinning. She fell back on the pillow in a delicious afterglow.

His blue eyes smoldered. *"Now, my love?"*

She shivered at the raw heat in his eyes. He kissed her hard, his breath coming fast. Then he eased her thighs apart and entered her with a moan. His long, slow thrusts built exquisite sensations that brought her closer to another climax. How strong he was, his muscles flexing as he moved. She was now an experienced married woman. Jason was the perfect lover, but she wanted to please him. That book of erotic drawings she'd found in the library at Deane Abbey was most helpful. She blushed as she murmured a suggestion in his ear.

He began to thrust harder, causing Beverly's thoughts to scatter. "That, my bewitching beauty," Jason lamented, "will have to wait!" He groaned. "At least until after luncheon."

About the Author

A USA TODAY bestselling author of Regency romances, with over 35 books published, Maggi's Regency series are International bestsellers. Stay tuned for Maggi's latest Regency series out next year. Her novels include Victorian mysteries, contemporary romantic suspense and young adult. Maggi holds a BA in English and Master of Arts Degree in Creative Writing. She supports the RSPCA and animals often feature in her books.

Like to keep abreast of my latest news? Join my newsletter.
http://bit.ly/1m70lJJ

Blog: http://bit.ly/1t7B5dx
Find excerpts and reviews on my website: http://bit.ly/1m70lJJ
Twitter: @maggiandersen: http://bit.ly/1Aq8eHg
Facebook: Maggi Andersen Author: http://on.fb.me/1KiyP9g
Goodreads: http://bit.ly/1TApe0A
Pinterest: https://www.pinterest.com.au/maggiandersen

Maggi's Amazon page for her books with Dragonblade Publishing.
https://tinyurl.com/y34dmquj

Printed in Great Britain
by Amazon